Green Watch

DOLPHIN'S REVENGE

Anthony Masters

Loner suddenly backed away from Anne, flipped round and took off at speed across the pool. To their horror, he swam full-tilt at the side and drove his head at the iron surround. There was a dull thump. He was thrown back slightly and paused – and then swam full-tilt at it again. The same dull thump echoed round the pool.

Tim is the newest member of Green Watch – an environmental pressure group founded by his uncle, Seb Howard, and his two kids, Brian and Flower. Together they battle to protect the natural world from ruthless exploitation – campaigning against the needless slaughter of innocent creatures and the thoughtless pollution of the environment. No animal is too small for Green Watch to care about and no place too remote for them to get to. Needless to say, they manage to ruffle quite a few feathers along the way . . .

DOLPHIN'S REVENGE

Book Three in the Green Watch series

by
ANTHONY MASTERS
Illustrated by Pauline Hazelwood

Hippo Books
Scholastic Publications Limited
London

Scholastic Publications Ltd.,
10 Earlham Street, London WC2H 9RX, UK

Scholastic Inc.,
730 Broadway, New York, NY 10003, USA

Scholastic Tab Publications Ltd.,
123 Newkirk Road, Richmond Hill,
Ontario L4C 3G5, Canada

Ashton Scholastic Pty Ltd.,
P O Box 579, Gosford, New South Wales,
Australia

Ashton Scholastic Ltd.,
165 Marua Road, Panmure, Auckland 6,
New Zealand

First published in the UK by Scholastic Publications Ltd., 1990

ISBN 0 590 76349 0

Typeset by AKM Associates (UK) Ltd., Southall, London
Printed by Cox and Wyman Ltd., Reading, Berks

To Penny Walker
who inspired the beginning
and
Anne Finnis who inspired
the rest.

Chapter One

The water was very clear and the wreck of the coaster was lying at the bottom of a rocky underwater valley. Tim could see the name on her bows very clearly: *Lodestar*. Her hull was covered in barnacles and she lay at a slight angle. There was a grey-green shimmer to her decks as a shoal of small fish wove their way out of one of the uncovered holds.

Tim shivered in his wet suit; there was something very sinister about the *Lodestar*'s grave. Her superstructure was covered in algae and drifting fronds of weed, and her wheelhouse was a dark gash in the undersea foliage whose strands formed a torn, sinuous curtain. What was in there? he wondered. A skeleton lashed to the wheel? Another still wearing a captain's hat, leaning in eternal vigilance against the bulkhead?

This was Tim's fourth dive off the Cornish coast in a week, and he could see Anne Dudley swimming just above him. She was the reason for Green Watch being here, and for Tim joining up with them again. It was months since all four members of Green Watch had been together in the South Atlantic, where they had nearly died at the hands of Captain Stanton and the murderous June Rose in their battle against the slaughter of the whales.* Tim had never been so frightened in his life, yet it had toughened him up and now he was finding the diving much easier than he had imagined.

He was also buoyed up by the knowledge that he had really been able to help Flower, Seb Howard's daughter, in the South Atlantic. Normally fearless and decisive, Flower had finally confided in him about her terror of the sea, and between them they had been able to conquer it. He could see her now, swimming alongside him, giving him a thumbs-up signal, while Brian, her brother, swam on his other side.

Seb, Tim's uncle, had stayed on land, trying to work out how Sam Jefferson and his dolphinarium were breaking the law. He was closeted with a lawyer Anne had found, but so far they had come up with nothing. This was why they were all together again; Anne was sure that Jefferson was mistreating his dolphins and hoped that Green Watch would be able to find some proof. But so far, despite many visits to

* Sad Song of the Whale

2

Dolphin World and many local enquiries, nothing had come to light.

Now, as Tim hovered over the wreck, he realised how dull life had been away from Seb, Flower and Brian. At first, when he had come home from the last assignment, Tim had been pleased to be safely back with Mum. His dad was in prison for fraud and life was difficult for all three of them, but Tim was really pleased that Dad took such an interest in his adventures. Talking about Green Watch had made prison visits so much easier. Unlike Mum, he had never expressed any fear about Tim's involvement with his brother Seb.

"He's given you something to live for all right, hasn't he?" he commented once.

It was more like having something to die for, thought Tim, for that was what they had nearly done on two, if not more, occasions during the last expedition. Anyway it was a curious phrase — "given you something to live for"; it was almost as if he were ill or something. Dad was coming out in six months and Tim wondered if he was anxious about that and worrying that they might not have missed him that much. In fact Tim had missed him dreadfully when he first went into prison, but Green Watch had given him so much loving human company as well as adventure that he now saw his father almost as a stranger, and was unsure of how to relate to him, particularly when he came out. He wondered if Mum felt the same. But then she had had no adventure, little human company and the continual worry of what he was doing with 'that brother of your dad's'. All she had as a companion was Rusty, the family dog, and although Tim knew she dearly loved him, she complained about him too. In fact she complained about everything, which perhaps wasn't very surprising, but it didn't make her easy to live with.

He felt a nudge on his shoulder. It was Anne. She was beckoning to him, beckoning him towards the wheelhouse of the wreck. There was something there – something coming out of the frond-strewn entrance.

It was the dolphin she had talked to them about earlier – the wild one. She had named him Loner, for although sometimes the dolphin seemed to want company, at other times he very clearly did not. To Tim Loner seemed absolutely enormous. His long, smooth body, pronounced beak and fin made him look sleek and streamlined, but it was his eye that really entranced Tim. It had a look of unwavering, inquisitive intelligence, and Tim stared back, almost unable to believe in what he was seeing.

Loner began to nose round Anne, making little darting playful dashes at her, but after a while he seemed to tire of this game and suddenly floated on to his back while she tickled him. Tim thought it amazing that he was a wild creature and yet so tame. But with equal rapidity, Loner swam away from her and shot towards the surface.

Anne signalled them to weave their way up slowly

in front of her; Brian first, then Tim, then Flower.

When Tim broke surface, he again felt the shock of the outside world. Around him were the dark cliffs of the Cornish cove. There was a short, choppy swell and riding it at anchor a battered motorboat that was Anne's most prized possession. Standing on the deck was one of the local fishermen's sons whom she employed over the weekends as part helmsman, part helper in her research into the habits of dolphins. He was good natured and enthusiastic and had a knowledge and love of the sea that Tim knew was born in him. He was fascinated by the dolphins and had told Tim how much he would miss them when he started work for a small boatbuilder over at Newquay. It wasn't really surprising; they were so lovely. Hanging on to the side of the boat Tim saw the fin on the surface and knew that it was Loner come back to play.

"How long's Loner been around?" asked Tim as they bounced back over the scudding sea. It was late August, at the end of a long, hot summer, and the air was warm and mellow.

"Oh – a long time." Anne was tall, with tumbling blonde hair that was bleached by the sun. Her skin was brown, so deeply tanned that it made her blue eyes very intense. When she talked Tim knew how passionately she felt about the dolphins – and how much she valued their freedom.

"They're like small whales," she said. "And they were once thought to be gods – Apollo would change into dolphin shape."

"They're mysterious," said Flower. "There's something about them that's so knowing – so intelligent."

"Isn't it true that in Ancient Greece they thought dolphins had once been men who had lived in cities? Not mortals, but more divine?" asked Brian.

Anne nodded. "There are no end of incredible legends associated with them."

"So it's a pity that Sam Jefferson bribes them with dead fish to perform." Brian's voice was edged with a deep anger. "Or worse," he added reflectively.

"It is worse," said Anne. "I'm sure he gives them electric shocks. That's why I'm here, living on this old boat and taking tourists out to dive to try and make ends meet."

So far Tim had not seen Jefferson's dolphinarium himself, and he wasn't sure that he wanted to either. "Don't they like music?" he asked.

"Yes, they love it. They're highly intelligent creatures – too intelligent to be exploited by Jefferson."

"What would happen if you released the dolphins he's got – out into the sea?" Tim wondered if she'd think him stupid but Anne smiled at him sympathetically.

"They wouldn't survive out here. I'm not sure whether all his were bred in captivity or imported or whatever, but in any case they would have forgotten how to survive in the wild."

"Isn't that instinct?" asked Flower.

"Not after they've been persecuted by Jefferson," she said angrily. "I want him closed – and the dolphins will have to go to a sanctuary. There's one in Devon."

"How do you know for sure that Jefferson ill-treats them?" asked Tim tentatively. "I'm not doubting your word, Anne, honestly. It's just that —"

"Am I simply being a hysterical dolphin-lover?" Anne finished for him.

"I didn't say that."

"No – sorry. I'm just being defensive. I know he does. I've known Sam Jefferson for a long time. We used to dive together. In fact he's a good diver and he could have stayed in diving if he hadn't been so greedy." She paused. "We went out to America – a whole bunch of us – and followed dolphins. He loved them as much as I did at one point. But that all changed and he came back here and started this business. All right –" She turned to Brian. "I don't know what your dad told you —"

"That you worked with him for a bit."

"OK, so you know I've been a complete fool —"

"Dad didn't say that," said Flower.

"Well, he should have. He has a lot of personality, has Sam, and I must have been half in love with him." She looked away from them, staring down at the wheel, her eyes full of angry tears. "I was so stupid. He convinced me that his dolphinarium would be different from the other ones; that the dolphins wouldn't be degraded. But he lied to me. They were just becoming zombies, learning to do

7

tricks all the time. So that was it. I got out. And now I'm not there I'm certain he's *really* ill-treating them, and I'm determined to stop him, to close him."

"When did you leave?" asked Tim.

"Over a year ago. I spent months trying on my own and got nowhere. I just couldn't produce any evidence. He was too careful. So I called Seb and asked him to bring Green Watch in. I know how resourceful you are." She smiled and immediately looked more relaxed. But Tim suddenly felt worried, as if he had picked up all the tension inside her.

Then he saw Loner.

He was to starboard, his dark torpedo-like shape a part of the water, cleaving gracefully through the waves. Then he dived and was lost to sight. Seconds later he re-emerged, jumping high out of the ocean in a great, elegant curve. Loner dived again – and jumped again – this time even higher. It was an incredible sight, the fading sunlight flashing on his mottled skin.

"He's fantastic!" said Tim.

Anne laughed. "He's showing off," she said affectionately.

A speedboat, travelling out from the harbour, headed towards them in a white curl of spume, while Loner continued to dive and to jump. Then, as the lashing speed of the boat neared him, Loner jumped again, but this time right over the bow of the

8

speedboat. It slowed down and headed towards them.

"It's Sam," said Anne quietly.

Sam Jefferson was wearing a sou'wester and oilskins. He had a wide, craggy, almost handsome face with a beard and a shock of startlingly white hair. He had a slight questioning smile on his face, and although he did not look in the least like a villain, there was a hardness in his eyes that seemed somehow out of place.

"Evening, Anne," he said as she cut her engines and the two boats bobbed up and down together on the swell.

"What do you want?" she asked brusquely.

"Doing a bit of dolphin-watching, are we?" As he said the words, Loner jumped over his bow again and then streaked off towards the open sea. "Fastest mover I've seen yet." He grinned fleetingly at Tim. "Quite sensational."

Tim stared back, not knowing what to say. Jefferson had an odd teasing way of speaking, and all the time he was talking to him, he was looking at Anne. "He'd make a star."

"You can't touch him," said Anne sharply. "He's protected."

"Is he?"

"He's protected by conservation laws. You can't take a wild dolphin."

"Who says I can't?"

"You'd be prosecuted."

"I can make him happy."

"Rubbish. Look what you've done to the others."

"Anne – you're a romantic."

"No, I'm a realist. And I'm going to run you out of business. Somehow."

"She gets a bit worked up, you know." This time Jefferson addressed Flower. "As I say – she's a romantic." He glanced goadingly back at Anne. But Flower was not going to play his game by answering. She simply turned her back on him. It was effective, for Tim caught a tiny trace of anger in Jefferson's eyes. Then it was replaced by a mocking glint. "Let battle commence." He laughed, but the sound was entirely without humour.

"Sam —" Anne began, a different note in her voice.

"Yes?"

"You're doing this to hurt *me*, aren't you? It's nothing to do with the dolphin."

"He's a fine specimen. That's all I'm interested in." Jefferson opened up the throttle of his speedboat and smiled. "I'll have him – you'll see. No one's going to know where I took him from." He roared away, the water glistening in a silver trough under the setting sun.

"Does he mean it?" asked Brian, breaking the desolate silence.

Anne nodded. "He means it all right."

Chapter Two

Green Watch were living in a caravan in a field just behind the harbour. When they arrived back Seb was outside, tending a barbecue.

"Hungry?"

"You bet!" they chorused.

He looked tired and his face was lined. When he relaxed, the lines seemed to go away, but at the moment he didn't seem very relaxed.

"Had a good dive?"

"It was fantastic!" said Flower. "And we saw the dolphin. Loner."

"Anne's dolphin." He smiled.

"She's very fond of it," Brian said quietly. "Maybe too fond of it."

"We met Jefferson," said Tim. "He says he's going

to catch it."

"Easier said than done," replied Seb. "Besides, he only said it to wind her up. Jefferson's a fool, but not a big enough fool to break the conservation laws."

"He looked a pretty competent fool to me," stated Flower bleakly.

"Yes," said Seb slowly. "And there's something else. I've been checking up on him. Local people mainly. The pub is the best grapevine. And I discovered something that, if it's true – and I think it is – is pretty disturbing."

"Why?" asked Tim excitedly.

"He's been inside. For violence. He nearly killed someone."

"Did Anne know him then?" asked Flower.

"No. When he came out. They were very close for a time. Shared interests – that kind of thing. They still are close in a way." He was passing round sausages and hamburgers.

"Close?" asked Tim incredulously. "They hate each other!"

"That's a kind of closeness," replied Seb. He bit into a sausage thoughtfully.

"Mum and you were like that," said Brian suddenly.

"Fair comment," returned Seb.

Tim glanced across at Flower. She looked away, but not before he saw the tears in her eyes. He should have kept quiet but something made him blurt out: "Do you ever see her now?"

"Occasionally," said Brian in a stilted voice.

"She's married to someone else now." He swallowed.

"When's your dad coming out?" Seb asked Tim gently.

"A few months."

"I've been thinking, if he wants a bit of a break, maybe he'd like to do something with us. After he's spent a bit of time with your mother, of course."

Tim could see that Flower was frowning at her father. But he was pleased at the offer. "I want you to meet him," he said, the words tumbling over each other. "I'm sure he'd love to come on one of our expeditions."

There was a slightly uneasy silence. Brian was the first to break it.

"Any progress?" he asked.

Seb sighed. "Not a lot – nothing to convict him. Just rumour and speculation. The only way we could be successful is to catch him actually maltreating his captive dolphins. And I still haven't thought of a way of doing that. Besides, Greenpeace has fought a magnificent battle in this country and almost won. The dolphinariums have to meet so many regulations now that most of them have gone out of business. Jefferson's only got a certain amount of time to put his house in order, and he'll never be able to afford to do that." He paused. "Of course that doesn't solve the present problem."

"Couldn't we break in?" asked Flower. "We've done it before."

"Maybe, but not in this case. I want to keep everything absolutely above board. I don't want

13

Jefferson to have *any* reason to score off us."

"Dad —"

"Yes, Brian?"

"There's a car coming. Fast."

Sam Jefferson's arrival in his sports coupé was as fast and dramatic as his earlier appearance in the speedboat. The car screeched to a halt on the grass a few metres away from the barbecue. When he got out, Jefferson looked much less genial than he had before. He was wearing a denim jacket and jeans, and in the gathering darkness his face was in shadow.

"Mr Howard?"

"Yes."

He glanced at Flower, Brian and Tim. "Oh, it's you lot again."

"Yes," said Flower. "It's us lot."

"What can I do for you?" asked Seb casually. "Fancy a sausage?"

"No thanks. All I want is you off my back."

"Sorry?"

"Keep out of my business."

"I've really no idea what you're talking about."

"You've been in all the pubs asking questions about me."

"I'm a curious man."

"And you've been trying to ruin my reputation."

"You've certainly got a poor one." Seb's voice was neutral. "Most people seem to think you ill-treat your dolphins."

"That's malicious gossip."

"Is it?"

14

"Spread by Anne Dudley – out of jealousy and spite."

"I can't agree with that."

"I don't care whether you agree or not. I've come to give you a warning. Clear out of here. Now. And take your kids with you."

"You threatening me?"

"I'm warning you that I won't tolerate the assassination of my character," he said pompously.

"Look, Mr Jefferson, I'm part of an environmental protection group called Green Watch. We're here to look into some complaints made about the running of your dolphinarium – and the source is irrelevant. Why don't you come clean and let me look around?"

"Because I don't choose to, and because I don't want evidence fabricated against me."

"There'll be no question of that."

"No?"

"No. Now why don't you —"

Jefferson walked right up to Seb and stood a few centimetres away from him. "Get out – or you'll be sorry."

"I'm not interested in threats."

"They're not just threats."

"What's that supposed to mean?"

"It means I'm a man of business, Mr Howard. I get what I set out to get. And I do not tolerate interference." He turned abruptly away, got into his car and roared off, churning up the grass.

"Well." Seb turned back to the barbecue. "He's not a very pleasant fellow, is he?"

"Is he all bluster?" asked Flower doubtfully.

"No. He seems to me to be a man at the end of his tether. I think he's extremely dangerous." Seb paused. "I don't want any of you going off on your own. We must stick together."

"But what are we going to do?" asked Brian. "We could be playing some really long waiting game."

"I suppose we could," replied Seb. "But why don't we go out tonight? Relax. See a show."

"A show?" said Brian, amazed that Seb had changed the subject so dramatically. "What kind of show?"

"How about seeing the dolphins perform?" he said. "We really ought to go and see for ourselves."

The building had once been a ballroom called *Spanish City* and the original architect had created a rather magnificent mock hacienda, with moorish towers and cupolas and even a slightly out-of-character dome. Bits had been added over the years and a tawdry shopping arcade occupied one side of the structure. On the other side red letters, dark in the night, advertised DOLPHIN WORLD.

"Well?" Seb joined a queue that stretched some way down the street. "Looks popular."

The others reluctantly joined him. "What happens if he won't let us in?" asked Anne.

"We shall stage an instant demonstration."

"You're in a militant mood, Dad," said Flower.

"I am. This campaign should really get home to

the ordinary person in the street. What Jefferson does is as cruel as the whalers are to the whales in a different sort of way. He may not kill them, but he degrades them totally. You'll see what I mean: making the dolphins jump through hoops, calling them Sammy and Bobby – destroying their dignity."

"It's like lions in a circus, isn't it, Seb?" put in Tim. "It makes them look silly, jumping through hoops."

"So if you don't like it – why you coming in?" asked a woman in a mac with a child on each hand.

"Research, madam," replied Seb. "Pure research."

As it turned out, they found no problem in being admitted, as Jefferson was nowhere to be seen. Once inside the rather shabby interior, Tim found himself looking down on the water in which half a dozen dolphins were ploughing lazily up and down. When the last of the audience had settled down, there was a fanfare of trumpets, the dolphins started leaping and a rich voice over the tannoy proclaimed, "Ladies and gentlemen, we give you one of life's true adventurers: deep-sea diver, ocean yachtsman, dolphin expert and dolphin lover – Mr Samuel Jefferson!"

He came on to a roll of drums, dressed in a sweat shirt with a dolphin on front and back, tracksuit trousers and beautifully whitened trainers. Jefferson bowed, climbed to a podium beside the pool and said into a handy microphone, "Ladies and gentlemen, boys and girls, welcome to Dolphin World – and to

17

the delights of my dolphins." He clapped his hands and the dolphins leaped in unison to applause.

Tim watched the rest of the show with mixed feelings. In a way it was entertaining; in another way it was degrading. The dolphins – Sammy, Bobby, Robbie, Timbo and Tommy – leapt around, jumped through hoops, jumped for toys, nosed balls, swam to ballet music, and for each of these acts received thunderous rounds of applause. Sam Jefferson looked rather splendid, athletic and full of jokes and praise for his dolphins. Yet, as the forty-five minutes or so drew to an end, Tim found himself suddenly angry, and when he glanced at the others, particularly Anne, he knew they were feeling the same. There was something about the contrast between the smug captivity of these performing dolphins, bouncing about in their pool, and Loner's unlimited freedom in the Atlantic. And when he thought of Jefferson's half-joking threat to end Loner's freedom, his anger increased.

Once the show had ended and they were all outside, Anne turned to them and said, "Well?"

Tim was first to speak. "It just made me so angry." He knew he was speaking for all of them.

Chapter Three

Tim knew what he had to do directly he went to bed that night. Ever since he had arrived in Cornwall, he had felt the urgent need to prove himself to Green Watch. It was not as if he hadn't fully participated in the last two adventures, but somehow, so much time had passed in between, that he felt desperate to make an impact again – to be important to them. What with his home situation compared to the unity and strength of the Howard family, Tim often felt very uneasy and desperately unsure of himself. He had proved himself in the past, but now was the time to do so again.

Suppose he broke into the dolphinarium? And took his camera? In the South Atlantic Seb had asked him to wear a special camera on his wrist so that he could photograph something secret on board a factory ship. But in this case, providing he was well hidden, he could use his own camera. The main thing was to find something important to photograph, like Jefferson being cruel to one of the dolphins.

Tim imagined himself striding into the caravan, instant prints in his hand, all showing the most incriminating evidence against Sam Jefferson. Surely that would wrap up the whole mission, and they could concentrate on diving with Anne and playing with Loner – who of course would be safe from Jefferson's clutches. Anne would be delighted, Seb would be delighted, Brian and Flower would be – He cautiously inched his way out of his bunk, which luckily was at the back of the caravan and nearest to the door. With equal caution he lifted the bolt and was out in the cool, fresh, night air. Tim looked at his watch. Just after one. And he was about to begin his very first solo mission.

Five minutes later, Tim's confidence was flagging. A light rain had started and he felt obvious – all too obvious – as he hugged the shadows of the stone wall and descended towards the town. Suppose he was stopped? What would he say? Just taking a walk? Needed a breath of fresh air? A number of explanations filled his mind, but all of them seemed inadequate.

But there was no one around, and gradually Tim's confidence returned. He looked towards the rain-pitted dark sea and thought of Loner out there somewhere, free and unafraid. Well, he was doing it for Loner too, wasn't he? A lump appeared in Tim's throat. What if Jefferson did manage to capture Loner and deprive him of his freedom? He just couldn't bear to think about him swimming around in that pool, watched by all those people. A circus act – no more. In fact Tim was concentrating so hard on avoiding the horrendous thought that he found he had arrived at the dolphinarium before he had realised it.

The building stood out, white and cold, in the light of the crescent moon. At first it seemed impenetrable. Then Tim noticed a passage that led between one side wall of the dolphinarium and the BEEFY HAM-BURGER BAR.

Nervously Tim began to edge his way down the narrow space, wondering where it would lead him. Then he saw that he was coming to the rear of the dolphinarium and that there was a yard at the back, surrounded by a fence that he knew he could climb. Without any hesitation he leapt for a handhold and was up and over the fence in a few seconds.

The yard was stacked with plastic barrels of what looked like salt, and there was a smell of fish. Looking up at the building Tim could see a garage with a flat roof. Once again he knew it would be easy to clamber on to it – and from there to an overhanging balcony. It was too easy, he told himself; he was too lucky. For a few moments he waited, wondering if he should play safe and clamber back over the wall. But two factors spurred him on, both of equal importance: proving himself and protecting Loner. Without any further hesitation, he began to pull himself up on to the roof of the garage, and from there to the balcony. He climbed noiselessly, and a few seconds later was peering through a window. He pushed it and it opened. Yes, surely it *was* too easy.

Stepping quietly over the sill, Tim found himself on another balcony, but this time looking inwards and downwards to the pool, surrounded by the banked seating. Then he froze. There was someone swimming.

It was some time before the shivering Tim realised that he was watching the fin of a dolphin lazily traversing the black water. Hurriedly, but still very softly, he clambered down an iron staircase until he was standing by the pool-side. His thoughts were hazy and suddenly he was blindingly tired. What was he going to do now he was inside? Hide somewhere? Wait for Jefferson to do something cruel? He patted his pocket – the camera was there all right. But supposing Jefferson did nothing cruel for days and days? And what would the Howards think when they missed him in the morning? Why hadn't he left them a note? He must have been mad.

But now the fatigue was overwhelming, and Tim looked desperately around for a hiding place where he could sleep. Behind him was a long corridor, and suddenly Tim was sure he could see a jerky movement. Something was sloping along, softly yet with a terrible alertness. Then he heard it panting, and seconds later saw its shape. It was a Rottweiler.

"Go away!" said Tim inside himself as he froze. "Go away!" But the dog came on. Now he could make out its jowls and its huge mouth in the half-light. It bared its teeth and gave a terrifying deep-throated growl. Tim backed away. There was only the pool behind him. Why hadn't he thought of guard dogs? Shouldn't there have been a notice? Fear made his thoughts become nonsensical. Still the Rottweiler came on, and still Tim backed away, till he could back away no further.

He could feel the dog's breath on his face now. It was foetid and warm. Absurdly, he was sure he could smell blood. The dog leapt as he back-somersaulted into the pool.

Tim hit the water with what seemed like a tremendous splash which echoed around the walls of the building. The vibration seemed to go on forever as he surfaced, spluttering. The water was stale and cold and very salty, with a hint of chlorine. Tim had swallowed some of it and held on to the side, choking. The dog began to bark. The dolphinarium echoed again to the hoarse sounds which went on and on, for the Rottweiler showed no signs of stopping. Then Tim felt a nudge – and then another. He looked down and saw the dolphin's eye. It reminded him of his mother, watching him in a hospital bed when he had had his appendix out. Then, above the barking, he heard the sound of footsteps, and before he could make any attempt to dive out of sight Sam Jefferson was there. He was grinning and there was not the

23

slightest trace of compassion in his eyes.

Jefferson knelt down by the pool, patting the dog who had at last stopped barking.

"Well!" he said in mock surprise. "What have we here?"

Tim said nothing.

"I'll call the police," said Jefferson, still patting the dog. "Shall I?"

Still Tim said nothing. He realised his camera was soaked, and his sense of failure was absolute. He hung on to the side of the pool without speaking, staring at Jefferson dumbly.

"Don't you speak?"

"Er —"

"Well?"

But Tim had nothing to say. Jefferson's eyes suddenly lit up. "I know you." He paused reflectively. "I definitely recognise you. You were in the boat, weren't you? In the boat with Anne Dudley."

Tim nodded dumbly.

"And you were by the caravan – with Howard. You're part of this ridiculous Green Watch outfit. Amateur do-gooders. Now get out of the pool!"

Tim eyed the Rottweiler uncomfortably. "What about —" he began.

"The dog won't hurt you."

"You sure?"

"Get out!"

Tim dragged himself out.

"I'm going to have you for breaking and entering my premises. They'll throw the book at you."

24

What would be worse? Tim wondered, the police or the wrath of Seb Howard? There was a lazy splash behind him and he saw that a couple of dolphins had swum over to look at what was going on.

As he stood up, shivering, the water cascading down him, his camera slipped out of his pocket and fell to the ground with a thud. He quickly retrieved it. Jefferson grinned.

"So – you were going to take some photos?"

"No."

"Why else would you bring in a camera at this time of night?"

"It was just in my pocket."

"Rubbish. I know what you were up to – I know what you were set up to do. They wanted you to take photographs, didn't they? In the hope that I kept this place like a tip, in the hope I was mistreating my dolphins. Well, you can see I don't. They're cared for. Right?"

"Right," said Tim. "But it wasn't Seb's idea, or Anne's."

"Don't give me that."

"It's true."

"Then who else could have put you up to it?"

"It was *my* idea."

"Rubbish!"

"It's true," Tim repeated impatiently.

"I'm going to call the police."

"Look —"

"Don't you try and talk your way out of this."

"Please. You *must* listen to me."

"The police will listen to you, for a nice long time, and then so will the magistrates." He turned away and marched back down the corridor. "Rocky will look after you."

Tim froze as he stared into the large, baleful eyes of the Rottweiler.

There had to be a way out. Tim lost eye contact with the dog and it growled. Supposing it sprang on him? Well, he could always dive back into the pool – if he could make it in time. The Rottweiler bared his teeth. They were enormous. The situation was hopeless. Then he had an idea.

The dog set up a horrible combination of howling and barking as Tim jumped back into the pool and began to swim towards a small bay. If only he had thought of it before – there must be a way out of the pool that the dolphins could take. If not, how could they be got out in an emergency? Or if the main pool was drained? He struck out across the cold, stale water. As he did so he could sense the movement behind him before he could hear it. One of the dolphins was beside him, nosing at him, almost edging him towards the bay. Once Tim was in it, he was in deep water that led to a grille. Hurriedly, he wrenched at the grille as the Rottweiler began to howl. For a moment, it was immovable. Then the grille lifted sharply upwards and he swam through. Would the dolphin follow? Tim thought it would, but no – it stayed behind him, watching, waiting, its eye unblinking.

Somehow he rammed the grille down behind him

and swam on, now in darkness. He was in a wide passageway and could see no end to it. Then he was up against another grille. Again he wrenched at it, it came up – and he was in another, much smaller pool. There was a nasty smell and, when he hauled himself up on the side, it was slimy and dirty and lined with old barrels. Shivering even more intensely, he turned round, looking for an exit. But he could see none at all. He stared back at the pool and caught sight of an object lashed to the side. It was a cage, tied with steel hawsers to the wall. The base stretched down under water. Then Tim saw the dark shape moving restlessly inside. It was a dolphin.

Despite the urgency of his situation, Tim knelt down and looked inside. The dolphin swam up to him until they were centimetres apart. He registered at once that its beak was broken and there were cuts, half-healed, on its head. But he had little time to notice anything else, for he suddenly realised the howling had stopped, to be replaced by the padding of feet and a harsh panting. Once again, Tim desperately sought a way out. But there were no doors anywhere, not even a window. There was only a narrow corridor at the end of which there was a door which he was sure led back into the main pool. But coming down the corridor was the Rottweiler, and the door behind it was open.

Without waiting, Tim threw himself back into the stinking water while the dolphin pushed hard at its bars. That must be the reason why its beak was so badly damaged, thought Tim. The dolphin must have spent hours hurling itself at the sides of its prison. Then the barking began all over again.

Jefferson walked slowly down the passage and, with equal casualness, strolled out to the grubby poolside.

"I see you've been for a swim."

Tim said nothing.

"Just exercise?" he said with irony, but there was something in his voice that had changed. He no longer sounded so confident, so self-assured.

"You've locked this dolphin up, and it's hurt itself."

"It's there for its own protection."

"Why?"

"It attacked another dolphin. That's how it got the injuries."

"I don't believe you."

"I don't care what you believe. The police will be here in a few minutes. Get out of that pool."

"No. I'm staying put. I want them to see all this – the dolphin and this filthy pool."

"This pool is out of use."

"Then what's this dolphin doing here?"

"I told you. Now get out. Fast."

"I'm staying put. You don't want me here, do you? You're frightened of what they might see." All the self-loathing at being caught was gone and Tim felt a new sense of resolution.

"Get *out*!"

"No chance."

"I'll send the dog in."

"Do that." Tim wasn't sure what the Rottweiler would do if he was ordered to go into the pool, but he was pretty sure that he wouldn't obey. After all, he could have gone in before.

"I'll have you out myself." Jefferson took off his shoes. "And if you get hurt in the struggle —"

"There won't *be* a struggle. You coward, you're twice my size – more."

Jefferson stood there hesitantly for a moment.

"You don't want them to see all this," said Tim. "Do you? I've found you out. It's like she said – you're mistreating them."

With a roar of anger, Jefferson waded into the pool. Tim waited for him to come.

"Got you!"

Tim shuddered as Jefferson grabbed him and began to drag him to the side of the pool.

"I'll tell them!" Tim yelled.

Jefferson seized him round the shoulders and forced his head below the water. He repeated the experiment several times and as Tim came up, struggling and gasping for air, he yelled into his face, "You're not telling anyone anything!"

"I am," sobbed Tim – and down he went into the scummy water again.

In the end, Jefferson dragged Tim out of the pool and half-carried, half-pushed him back down the corridor, through the passage into the main, dimly lit pool.

"I'll tell!" Tim kept repeating as he spat out water. "I'll tell!"

Without warning the two uniformed policemen walked on to the surround. One was quite young, the other older with a kind face. It was the kind one who spoke, and Tim quickly realised that his looks belied him.

"Now then, what have you been up to, lad?" he barked, his voice thin and cold.

"He broke in here," said Jefferson, "and jumped into the pool to avoid Rocky."

The Rottweiler was just behind them, panting quietly.

"I should think he did," observed the young policeman, but his companion frowned.

"Well?"

Tim stuttered a reply. "He keeps the place filthy – and he's cruel to the dolphins."

"That's no reason for breaking in." The policeman's cold logic was effective; Tim almost agreed with him, and he was sure Seb would. But he stumbled on desperately.

"You look at the other pool, down that passage. There's a dolphin – in a cage – and battered."

"It attacked one of the others," said Jefferson smoothly, "and got more than it bargained for. The vet recommended isolation."

"It's filthy in there," continued Tim doggedly.

"So you broke into the premises to —"

"I was going to take photographs." Tim produced his sodden camera. "Show him up."

"Of course he's been put up to it," said Jefferson.

"Who by?"

"Some amateur conservation group that are camped out in that field overlooking the harbour. Character named Seb Howard – he uses kids."

"Uses?"

"Gets them keen, and then gets them to run amok. Got his own family at it."

"He never told me to do anything," insisted Tim. "He doesn't even know I'm here." The situation was getting worse now that Seb had become involved. Tim had a sudden vision of Green Watch falling apart, all because of him. He had set out to try and prove himself to them, and now he had probably dealt them a mortal blow.

"We'll look into that," said the policeman ominously. "I think we'd better go and see this man Howard right away. But first of all you can tell me your name."

"Tim Howard."

"Address?"

He gave it, and as he did so he had a painful vision of his mother hearing the news of his arrest, and eventually his father hearing it in prison.

"And now, son," said the kindly-faced but icy-voiced policeman, "before we have a chat with Mr Howard – just tell me first of all how you broke in, and also how you came to be staying in that caravan."

Gulping, the tears beginning to squeeze out of his eyes, Tim began to tell him.

31

Chapter Four

"Mr Howard?"

Seb stood by the caravan door looking dishevelled. It was 7am and he had not expected to be woken so early. The policeman had his hand on Tim's shoulder in an almost benevolent way.

"Tim —" Seb was very disconcerted. "You should be in bed."

"He was up and about, I'm afraid, sir."

"Why?"

"Couldn't tell you. He broke into the dolphinarium. Mr Jefferson – the owner – he caught him and phoned us. We'll be charging the boy with breaking and entering."

"I don't believe it!" Seb's face was almost comic in his disbelief.

"It's a fact, sir. The boy's made some wild accusations – says he broke in to get some photographs of how Jefferson ill-treats his dolphins. But as you can see he's a little wet and so is his camera."

"Tim, is all this true?"

He nodded. "I didn't think we'd get any evidence, so I took a risk. It didn't pay off."

"And the photographs?"

"I had to jump in the pool. Jefferson's got this Rottweiler and it was the only place he wouldn't follow me. Trouble is, I got the camera wet so it's useless. But he *is* ill-treating them, Seb. I saw this dolphin all battered – in a cage."

"That makes no difference," replied the policeman.

"You're an idiot, Tim! What are you?"

"An idiot, Seb."

"You've done us an awful lot of harm – you know that?"

"Yes."

"You could have killed off our chances of operating here."

"I'm sorry." Tim wished he could die. Here and now. On the ground in front of the caravan steps. He had ruined everything. Rather than pulling off a coup for Green Watch, he had dragged them into disgrace. He had not felt so low since his father had been arrested.

"It's too late to be sorry, Tim." Seb rubbed it in even harder and then turned to the policeman. "What's the next step, officer?"

"You had better accompany me to the police station," he said. "Are you the boy's legal guardian?"

"Er, no. But his mother could be contacted. Except she's in London . . ."

"You'd better come down for the moment, sir," said the policeman reluctantly. But they were interrupted by the frantic appearance of Anne Dudley. Tim had never seen her so upset. She came running towards Seb, completely oblivious of the police.

"He's gone!"

"What? Who's gone?"

"Loner!"

"He can't have." Seb was totally bewildered.

"He's gone! Nowhere to be seen – I've checked everywhere."

"Maybe he swam out to sea."

"No – the tide's wrong."

"Look, Anne —"

"I tell you it's true. He's gone!" She suddenly stared at the policeman as if she had not seen him before. "Officer, you've got to help me! A dolphin's been taken."

The policeman turned on Tim as if he had it tucked down his shirt. "You been nicking fish?"

"Of course I haven't."

By this time Flower and Brian had emerged sleepily from their bunks and were standing on the steps, trying to make out what was going on.

Anne looked in astonishment and frustration from Tim to his captor then to Seb and back again. "What are you talking about?"

"A dolphin, madam. You say it's been stolen. From the dolphinarium."

"From the where? Of course not. From the sea. But I'm sure Jefferson's behind it."

"How could he steal a dolphin from the sea?" asked the policeman, now as bewildered as Anne. "It's this lad who's been breaking and entering."

But Anne wasn't listening. She was beside herself, desperately appealing to Seb now. "What are we going to *do*?"

"I'll come out in the boat with you, directly I've sorted out Tim."

"What's he done?"

"Broke into the dolphinarium."

"Because he thought Loner was there? Well done, Tim. Was he there?"

She looked almost crazily at him as Seb bellowed: "For God's sake – everyone calm down!"

"I'm very calm, sir," said the policeman indignantly. "It's the young lady who's —"

But Seb could stand no more. "I want to sort this out!" he yelled. "Like now."

Tim was charged with breaking and entering but was returned to Seb's safekeeping before coming up in front of the Juvenile Court the following Friday – in five days' time. By midday they were on windswept water, heading out in Anne Dudley's boat towards Loner's playground.

As they tossed and rolled through the waves, Tim

sat alone, miserable and afraid. Although he was concerned about Loner, he was also concerned about himself and, more than that, the way he had let Green Watch down. What was more, he had been nicked, just like Dad, and was coming up in court, again just like Dad. What would Mum think? And more important, what would she say?

Seb had said very little to him driving down to the harbour, and Flower and Brian had been unusually sudued. Only Anne Dudley's mind was on other things; she hardly seemed to register anything except the disappearance of Loner. Seb had tried to ring Mrs Howard from the police station but there had been no reply, for which Tim was deeply thankful, although he realised that he was only putting off his mother's fury and disappointment.

The spray coursed the deck, flying into Tim's face. He was grateful for it. The cleansing effect made him wild and angry. Didn't they realise all the risks he had taken for them? Didn't they know how hard he had tried when none of them had any ideas at all? That was the trouble with Green Watch, he thought. They were the Howard family, smug and disapproving, and he was a mere hanger-on. The fatigue grew in him but he was determined not to show it. His anger increased. Then, as he sat rigidly in the bows of the fiercely rocking boat, Tim felt a tug on his arm. It was Seb.

"Yes?"

"I want to talk."

"There's nothing to say. I messed it up."

"Yes."

"So what is there to talk about?" Tim felt the hard knot of anger contract and reach out inside him. It was like a living thing.

"Why it happened. What we're going to do."

"I wanted to catch him. That's all."

"By doing something illegal yourself?"

"I was going to take photographs. I could have photographed that caged dolphin. Aren't you interested? And why aren't we there now, showing the police?"

"Because if he's got any sense at all, he'll have hidden the cage and released the dolphin. And he *has* got sense. Unlike you."

"Thanks. How else would we have seen the cage?"

"I don't know."

"Eh?"

"I tell you – I don't know. But I do know we can't break in."

"We trespassed on that whaling ship to get photos."*

"Sure, but that was in the middle of the South Atlantic. You can't do that here and get away with it. You've got to learn the difference."

"I've learnt it – don't worry."

"I shall speak for you in court – and don't forget, Juvenile Courts aren't reported."

"What will happen?" asked Tim fearfully.

"You'll be bound over – I hope."

* Sad Song of the Whale

37

"What's that mean?"

"Let off. With a warning."

"And Mum?"

"She could be difficult. I can't fight *her*, Tim."

"You mean she might insist on me going home?"

"She might."

"I won't go."

"You can't stay here without her permission." Seb's voice was firm.

"Please —"

"So we'll have to convince her."

"Can we?" Tim looked at him, clutching at a tiny speck of hope. "What do you mean?"

"I mean what I say. I'll call her when we get back. Try to make her see sense."

"Sense?"

"The sense of your staying with me."

"Do you really want me?" asked Tim miserably.

"Yes – we all make mistakes. We want you all right."

"And Flower and Brian?"

"Of course they do. You *know* they do."

"I've let you down."

"Don't be self-pitying!" Seb snapped. "I can't stand that."

"But it'll go against Green Watch."

"So what? There've been plenty of things that've gone against us before, and we've ridden them." Seb put his arm round him, squeezing his shoulders hard. "You've got guts, Tim."

"I have?" Suddenly some of the unbearable weight lifted.

"Misdirected guts in this case. Did you feel you had to prove yourself? Just because of the gap since you were with us last?"

Tim nodded.

"Then you're a fool. You didn't have to prove anything – not after what's happened in the past. You've proved yourself already. Forever."

"But you're a family. Green Watch is a family."

"You feel left out?" asked Seb gently.

"A bit."

"We may be a family," Seb's voice pierced the noise of the wind and waves, "but you're part of it."

Tim felt a warm glow and an unbearable tightness in his throat. He looked away as the tears splashed down his face, but Seb's grip on his shoulders was firm.

The wind grew stronger as Anne circled her rackety old boat around the cliffs. The waves occasionally lashed over the prow and seagulls swooped down, seemingly enjoying the chaos of the increasingly bad weather. And as the sea increased the waves mounted until they lashed the cliffs in spumes of spray.

"He's probably sheltering," said Flower.

"Loner *never* shelters," snapped Anne. "Never. He loves storms. He rides them – like he'd ride the wind if he could. Someone's taken him, or he's dead."

"He can't be dead!" yelled Tim over the wind. Despite everything, he felt part of them again and he also felt an increasingly blind faith in Seb and his influence on the courts and his mother. Now his concern was for Loner.

"It's getting heavy," muttered Anne as she fought the tiller. "We don't want to be broached to out here."

"Give it another run." Seb sounded confident.

They did, chugging, wallowing, sometimes hurtling along the base of the cliffs while the spray showered over them. Tim looked at the gaunt rocks in apprehension. Anne was obviously a skilful navigator and she knew the coast well. It was not so much the cliffs that terrified him but the razor-sharp rocks in the sea, green and black in the foaming tumult of white-crested waves.

"We'll have to run back to the harbour," she said. "I don't want to put you all in danger."

She turned the boat out to sea in a wide arc. Just as they were about halfway through the turn, there was a dull and mournful sound from somewhere round the corner of the towering cliffs.

"What the hell's that?" demanded Flower.

"It's a maroon." Seb's voice was grim.

"There's a ship aground," Anne cursed. "Probably up on Dragon's Teeth just round the corner. They're vicious."

"What about the lifeboat?" asked Tim as another dull whine was heard over the sea.

"They'll be on their way. But we should go,"

rapped Anne. She turned to Seb. "What do you think?"

"Can *we* ride this out?"

"I don't know. I've never had her out in weather like this before."

"Then we'll have to see —"

"You mean —"

"Get her prow up again. We'll chance it. We could save lives."

"In this?" said Flower.

"In anything," Seb replied firmly. He turned to Tim and said softly, "There you are – I'm chancing my luck now. Let's hope it holds out better than yours."

He grinned and ruffled Tim's hair.

As they rounded the corner, Flower gasped and shouted out, "Oh, God – look at her!"

It was a large trawler, her nose seemingly buried in a mass of jagged rocks – the well-named Dragon's Teeth. She was tilted over at an alarming angle and sea was cascading over her decks in spumes of angry white water. Between waves Tim could just make out the name on her bow: the *Pole Star*.

There were men on her decks and some of them were unsuccessfully trying to launch a rubber dinghy. Another maroon went up as a terrible grinding, rending sound came from deep inside the ship.

"She's breaking up!" yelled Seb.

41

"They'll never get that dinghy launched – the wind's against them!" Anne shouted back.

"Can we get near them?"

"From the other side – yes."

"Can you make it?"

"Maybe. It's a risk."

"Take it."

"What about the kids?"

"Will those guys on that trawler last until the lifeboat gets out here?"

The rending, tearing sound came again.

"No, I don't think so. It's deep water and she'll go straight down if she tears herself off those rocks."

"Then we'll have to go in – they'll never survive in these seas."

"OK."

"Can you get a line on?"

"Maybe."

It seemed to take hours to bucket their way to the other side of the *Pole Star* and as they churned and shuddered through the crests, the men on board were still trying to launch their dinghy.

"It's her death throes," said Brian as more rending sounds came from the heart of the trawler.

Anne picked up a megaphone from the cramped wheelhouse. "I don't know if they'll hear me."

"Try. Now. I think we're getting to the eye of the storm – to a bit of calm. It won't last long!" shouted Seb. Sure enough, it did look to Tim as if the wind was beginning to abate slightly, and with it the size of the waves. Instead, the swell looked oily, heaving

42

against the side of the *Pole Star* in a sultry, stubborn sort of way.

"Ahoy, *Pole Star*! Ahoy, *Pole Star*!"

A man ran down the deck of the stricken ship towards them. He also had a megaphone in his hand.

"Ahoy, *Lady Lucy*!"

"We could try to get a line aboard!"

"Can't hear you!"

"We could *try* to get a line aboard!"

The man turned to someone else on the spray-hung deck and then shouted back into the megaphone.

"It's impossible!"

"He's right." Seb glanced at the mounting waves. "We've passed the centre – it's building up again."

Suddenly Tim noticed something familiar on the cluttered, sloping deck of the trawler.

"Seb —"

"What is it?"

"There's a cage —"

"A what?"

"A cage on the deck. Look – it's half in and half out of that rubber tank."

Anne's eyes were instantly riveted to the *Pole Star* and Tim had never seen such sudden, intense loathing. "You mean they've got Loner up there?"

"If they have, he could be back in his natural element very soon," said Flower drily.

"But he'll be trapped —"

"Hang on." Seb was shielding his eyes against the spray. "You're assuming a lot, aren't you? We've no

43

idea if there's *anything* in that cage." They all started talking at once but Seb cut them short. "I think I can see the lifeboat," he said thankfully.

Tim had never seen a lifeboat in action before. It was an extraordinarily splendid sight as it lanced through the waves. The crew in their sou'westers crouched in the bows, looking just like a posse in a Wild West film coming to relieve a beleaguered force, while the men scrambling about on the crazily tilting, groaning carcass of the *Pole Star* were like helpless ants, running about and achieving nothing.

The lifeboat swung round the rocks in a wide curve and the bosun signalled to Anne to stand off.

"They'll be in radio contact with the *Pole Star*!" Seb yelled. "Back off!"

Unwillingly Anne pulled the tiller over and the boat wallowed away from the *Pole Star* while the lifeboat manoeuvred her way in.

"They've got Loner," she whispered, almost to herself. "They've got Loner. I'm sure of it. The lifeboat'll have to get him off."

The crew of the *Pole Star* had been struggling to untangle a huge, thick net, and now they were trying to run it over the side of the listing ship. Finally they succeeded and it flapped down the rusty, wave-battered steel.

"They've got to get him off!" shouted Anne. "I've got to tell them!"

"Wait," said Seb. "Let them get off first."

"Why?"

"Because to ask questions about a cage over a

44

megaphone at a time like this could be distracting and highly dangerous. And in the end, men's lives are more important than a dolphin's!" he snapped.

But she wasn't convinced. "Are they? I couldn't agree less."

"And the weather's worsening. Again."

"So what?"

"The children."

"They're your responsibility —" She hardly knew what she was saying, so desperate was she about Loner's fate.

"Anne – for God's sake!"

"I *must* contact them!"

"No. We should turn round – go back to harbour. There's nothing we can do."

"Please, Seb —" They were screaming at each other in the wind. Neither could hear anything but they both knew exactly what was being said.

"Dad, let her try." Flower was adamant and in the midst of everything Tim felt a flash of pride that she had put her fear of the sea so positively behind her.

"The weather's too heavy for this little boat. We'll capsize." Seb's voice was urgent and determined.

"Please —"

"It's going to take them quite a while to get those men off. By that time they might have to rescue us, and put everyone's lives at risk. Do you understand, Flower? Anne?" It was the first time Tim had ever seen Seb at a loss. Somehow he had always been able to come up with a solution and Tim realised with a sudden shock that he had never expected to see him beaten.

Slowly Anne nodded, and with a despairing glance at the deck of the *Pole Star* she turned the boat back to shore. Meanwhile, the first man from the trawler was struggling down the net to the lifeboat below, and as they bounced past, one of the lifeboat men raised a hand in thanks and farewell.

Tim watched the listing trawler grow smaller until it was lost in poor visibility. The wind had reached new heights and the waves rose steeply, crashing water into *Lady Lucy*, threatening to sink her at any moment.

"Bale!" yelled Seb. "But put a line on first."

They clipped on safety lines and left the claustrophobic snugness of the wheelhouse for the small, vulnerable open deck. It had a well which was gradually filling with water. Armed with buckets and continuously battered by wind and waves, Tim, Flower and Brian fought to bale out. But it was a hopeless task, and as Tim looked up he could see great swollen clouds racing across the sky. Thunder boomed a few miles away, while flashing lightning occasionally lit the wreck of the *Pole Star* dramatically in an icy blue light which was tinged with purple. She looked even more at an angle now, as if she would slide down into the sea at any moment. Her nose had reared up and the rest of her was bent away from the rocks, while the long fingers of the lashing, foaming waves reached out to drag her down into the depths.

Tim kept glancing at Anne, knowing the anguish in her heart, and the other members of Green Watch did the same. But Anne only stared miserably ahead; she did not dart one glance behind her at all.

Chapter Five

Later that afternoon, having showered and rested, Brian came out into the field to see Tim and Flower gloomily playing cards. Seb had gone off, not telling them where he was going, and there was an atmosphere of restless anticlimax. The wind had dropped and there was a kind of battered, exhausted stillness.

"You know what I reckon," he said softly.

"What?" asked Tim moodily.

"Those two are out there."

"What?" Flower leapt up.

"Dad and Anne."

"No."

"They fooled us."

She was furious. "That's so rotten."

"They thought it was too dangerous for us,"

pronounced Brian dismissively.

"It's the first time." Flower's voice was hollow. "They're beginning to leave us out."

"They thought it was too dangerous," agreed Tim, knowing he sounded feeble. A couple of hours' sleep, however, had worked wonders with him. He felt great. Somehow, the misery of how he had let everyone down had receded and the blind faith he had in Seb had returned and was beginning to act as a screen against reality.

"Oh, yeah?" Brian, usually so patient and thoughtful, now sounded quite aggressive. "He *never* leaves us out."

"Let's go down to the harbour and meet them," said Tim, trying to cheer them up.

"OK," replied Flower. "Let's do that. But the reason I'm going down is to make a protest."

"Same here," said Brian angrily.

The harbour was as strangely silent as the caravan site; it seemed as if all the elements were exhausted, utterly spent. There was no sign of *Lady Lucy* but a number of trawlers were drawn up by the quayside. They were deserted. Stone houses, a pub and some drying sheds clustered round the stone walls that guarded the sheltered harbour, and there was a smell of weed and fish and the kind of sea-freshness that comes after a storm.

"We'll wait," said Flower grimly.

"OK," replied Tim, sitting on the wall and picking

up some stones. Absentmindedly he threw them at an old box on the beach, and one accidentally hit Brian's foot.

"You idiot —"

"Sorry."

"That hurt." He advanced on him threateningly but Tim still sat on the wall. He was curious; he had never seen Brian in a temper before. Suddenly Tim realised how badly the Howard children had been hurt – how much it meant to them to be left behind.

"I said I was sorry."

"Leave it, Brian," said Flower.

"He's a clumsy oaf!"

"Push off!" muttered Tim, stung by Brian's rudeness.

"What?"

"I said – push off!"

"I'll sort you out!" Brian was centimetres away from him now.

"Look, you two, don't make things worse," hissed Flower, conscious of the unloading of a whole coach-load of tourists near the quayside.

"Just because I let you down!" snarled Tim.

"I didn't even mention it!" rapped Brian.

"You were thinking it though!"

"Rubbish!"

"I know you were!"

"If you *really* want to know, I was feeling sorry for you, that's all."

"You patronising —" Tim launched himself off the wall at Brian and they fell on to the hard pebbles, rolling and punching and kicking, watched resignedly by Flower.

"There's another cage on that trawler," she said abruptly.

Tim got up and tried to help Brian to his feet, but he pushed him away fiercely.

"A what?"

"Look on the deck. I just noticed while you two were trying to kill each other."

Brian and Tim looked at the deck of the trawler that was nearest to them. Sure enough, there was a cage and a large, deflated plastic pool.

"Another one!" gasped Brian, brushing himself down.

"What are we going to do?" asked Tim helplessly.

"Board her. What else?" snapped Flower.

As they walked along the jetty, Tim said to Brian, "I'm sorry about that."

"It was my fault, Tim," said Brian awkwardly. "I was so angry about Dad – him leaving us like that. I took it out on you. Friends again, OK?"

"Yeah. OK."

They arrived at the end of the jetty. The trawler was moored to another one and they would have to cross a boat to get to her.

"So we can be done for trespass twice," muttered Brian. "Isn't this the same as breaking and entering?" He glanced uneasily at Tim, who looked quickly away.

"If it is," said Flower, very firmly, "then it's just too bad."

51

"Flower!" Brian was horrified.

"What?"

"You can't just walk on to that boat."

"Why not? There's no one around."

"You *can't*," whispered Tim. "Look what happened to me. We don't want all three of us in court."

"I'm taking the risk."

"No!" Brian was adamant.

"You two stay here and keep watch. I'm going aboard." And without further discussion she stepped on to the first of the trawlers with a very positive air, rather as if she owned it.

"Flower —" Brian was desperate.

"Shut up - and keep watch!"

"There's only about fifty tourists coming."

"Too bad. They won't know."

She was on the second trawler now, bending over the deflated pool.

"What if the owner comes back?" hissed Tim.

"Too late now," replied Brian woodenly.

It was some time before Flower returned. Miraculously, no one had arrived to question why she was on the trawler, although she must have spent over five minutes snooping about on the deck and staring into the wheelhouse. Eventually, rather reluctantly, she came back.

"What's up?" asked Tim.

"Nothing."

"But —"

"There's this sort of wire cage thing and a pool big enough to keep a dolphin alive, I should think. But there's no sign of anything."

"So there was one on the wreck, and another on this one. It's like a hunting party," said Brian.

"The point is, were they successful?" wondered Flower.

"Let's go to the lifeboat station," said Tim, making up everyone's mind. "They'll know who owns the boats – and maybe a bit more."

"Good idea," replied Brian warmly and even Flower, plunged into despair by her useless quest, said:

"Tim —"

"Yeah?"

"We've all made mistakes. It was a good cause – don't let it worry you. Dad will sort it out somehow."

"I know," said Tim, but secretly he wondered how Seb could sort it out. He had been shaken by the doubt he had sensed in Seb when they were out by the wreck.

"And one more thing." Flower's voice broke into his thoughts.

"Yeah?"

"You're a great member of Green Watch, Tim!"

"Thanks."

"The point is," said Brian, "we all have to take risks. Some pay off – others don't. And I'll tell you – we're going to have to take a lot more."

53

"Yes, son?"

The lifeboat man was young – only a few years older than Brian.

"Did they all get off the wrecked trawler? We were on the *Lady Lucy*, just standing by."

Tim and Flower stood in silence, letting Brian do all the talking.

"You were pretty close."

"We thought we'd have to rescue them, if you lot hadn't turned up."

"Well, we did. Pretty quick and all. We had the call directly those maroons went up. We got 'em all off and they've gone home. Didn't need any hospital treatment or anything." He looked at them, all smiling triumph.

"We noticed something funny on the deck of the *Pole Star*."

"Eh?"

"Kind of cage thing and a pool – an inflatable pool."

"Didn't see that – we were concentrating on the rescue."

"Of course you were. Just wondered what it was for."

"Couldn't tell you."

"There's another one – over there."

"Over where?"

"There – on that trawler with the blue wheel-house."

"The *North Star*?"

"Yeah."

54

"A cage, you say, and a pool? An inflatable?"

"That's it."

"Never seen anything like that before. Must have a purpose though. Now —" He was obviously anxious to get on.

"Don't know who owns it, do you?"

"The two *Stars*? They're sister ships. Or were – I don't know if the *Pole*'s gone down yet."

"No point in salvage?"

"There won't be nothing left to salvage."

"So —"

"The owners. Roddy and Alec Winter. Brothers, they are. Been fishing for years. They used to have the two boats. Still —" He paused. "Guess the insurance will take care of that."

"Do you know where they live?"

"Whitewood Lane - just turn right out of the harbour. Number twelve. But don't you go bothering them today. Not after what happened."

"Of course not," said Brian. "I'll probably write to them."

"What about?" At last he was more curious.

"I was just interested —"

"Oh, them trap things. OK. Don't go taking that boat of yours out in bad weather again. Wouldn't like you to lose it."

"No," said Brian. "We won't - we'll be careful."

They strolled out into the mellow early evening sunlight. Still *Lady Lucy* hadn't returned.

"What the hell are they doing?" asked Brian, looking really worried.

"Searching for Loner," said Flower. "You know how Anne feels. Look, I'll go and see these Winters."

"Hang on," replied Brian. "I'll go."

"No."

"Why not?"

"Because you've done your share. And so has Tim. Now it's my turn."

"I've done nothing," said Brian.

"I'm going." She was determined.

"Wait a minute —" Tim looked towards the *North Star*. "There's somebody on board her."

"Excuse me."

"Yes?"

He was stocky and brutish-looking, with a cap and thick jersey, despite the warmth of the evening. Flower had calmly boarded the *North Star* again. Dimly the boys could hear her from the quayside.

"Are you Mr Winter?"

"What if I am?"

He was actually dismantling the cage, separating it from the deflated pool.

"Are you the owner of this trawler?"

"I'm a partner in it. Why?"

"We were out when the *Pole Star* went down – trying to help before the lifeboat came."

"Oh, yeah? What vessel were you?"

"*Lady Lucy*."

"My brother mentioned it. Thanks for standing

by." He was gruff, faintly suspicious rather than grateful.

"Is he all right?"

"He'll be fine. Alec's resting."

"I'm glad." She paused casually. "They had one of those on board."

"Eh?"

"That cage thing."

"Oh, yeah?"

"What's it for?" asked Flower with attempted innocence.

"What's it to you?"

"Just wondered."

"Well – wonder away."

"I —"

"It ain't no business of yours, is it?"

"No."

"So – you did a good job out there. You stood by Alec and for that we're grateful. Now I'm busy."

"OK. Goodbye." Flower walked quickly over the boat and back to the jetty. She shrugged as she came up to them, but Brian was looking out to sea.

"*Lady Lucy*'s coming in," he said.

"What are you lot up to?" was Seb's first question as they helped to tie up *Lady Lucy*.

As Flower explained Anne's face seemed to grow grey and her tan disappeared.

"Oh, God!"

"It may not mean anything," said Seb.

"What about the *Pole Star*, Dad?" put in Brian.

"She's broken up and gone down."

57

"What have you been doing?" asked Tim.

"Searching for Loner," replied Anne, her voice expressionless.

"Any luck?"

"No."

Seb watched Roddy Winter working on the *North Star*. He had dismantled the cage and had put it in one of the holds. Now he was folding up the inflatable.

"They either got him," he muttered, "or they're giving up. And if they did —"

Brian got there at the same time. "He either went down and is still trapped in the wreck of the *Pole Star* or he's in the dolphinarium. Jefferson's got him."

Tim thought again of the dim, dark, dirty pool with its brackish water. He shuddered. Could a dolphin die of fear? "What do we do?" he asked inadequately.

"Let's get down there." Flower seemed determined to do everything immediately.

"He's done it to hurt me, that's all." Anne stood staring into the town, beyond the harbour, where the dome of Dolphin World could just be seen. "He wanted to take away the one – the one thing I loved more than anything else. More than him. I suppose he was jealous."

"Maybe." Seb was impatient, frowning at Flower, who was practically jumping up and down in despair at the delay. "But we don't even know if Loner's in there yet."

"He's not allowed to take him out of the sea," said Tim. "He's breaking the law."

"If he *has* taken him, he is," Seb assured him. "But we've got to prove it."

"The cage – the inflatable —" Brian began.

"Sure. It's our word against theirs. And with Tim coming up in court . . ." Seb's voice tailed away. Anne sighed and Tim wished he could fade away on the spot. Because he had been so stupid it looked as if Loner would be a captive forever.

"What are we going to *do*?" he asked Seb again, this time desperately.

"There's only one way to find out about that dolphin," replied Seb, "and that's to confront Jefferson."

"But he won't tell us anything, will he?" asked Brian.

"He probably will if we threaten him with the law."

"What are we waiting for?" yelled Flower.

Chapter Six

"I want to see Mr Jefferson."

"I'm afraid he's not available." The woman behind the box office window looked at her watch. "He's doing the last show. It's after nine, you know." She sniffed disapprovingly, eyeing the five scruffy and tired-looking people as if they ought to be in a dosshouse.

"Then we'll wait," said Seb, sitting down on the torn plastic of a bench seat. The others spread themselves around restlessly. Tim went to look at the posters. One read:

DOLPHIN WORLD
MARVEL AT THE WORLD'S MOST
INTELLIGENT CREATURES

THEY JUMP
THEY DIVE
THEY SOMERSAULT
THEY PERFORM ACROBATICS
YOU WON'T BELIEVE YOUR EYES

Another read:

World-famous professional diver, Sam Jefferson, has swum with dolphins for many years. Because he believes in the wild and in conserving the world dolphin population, Sam only trains and exhibits dolphins born in captivity.

"Hey!" Tim was beside himself with rage. "Look at this!"

They gathered round noisily while the box-office lady sniffed disapprovingly again.

"What do you reckon, Dad?" asked Brian.

But it was Anne who answered. "He's got him all right. Partly to spite me, partly as some kind of challenge. I honestly think he believes these dolphins are happier with him than anyone. And he's determined to prove it with Loner." She looked back at the posters. "These dolphinariums – there's so much legislation going through at the moment that it's going to cost them a fortune to keep open."

The box-office lady sniffed disapprovingly again, but Anne carried on regardless.

"They're going to have to enlarge the pools, provide better —" She broke off mid-sentence as Jefferson appeared. He looked very confident.

"There are some people here to see you, Mr Jefferson," said the box-office lady, looking at Anne as if she had just been sick on the floor.

"Yes," said Sam Jefferson. "I know them." He smiled politely. "Would you like to see round?" he asked smoothly.

They walked into the deserted main pool. The half dozen dolphins glided about the surface lazily. They had none of Loner's liveliness, thought Tim, as he watched them swimming around lethargically.

"Where have you put Loner?" demanded Anne immediately.

"I don't go in for collecting wild dolphins," Jefferson said casually. "Not personally."

"What's that meant to mean?" she asked. "Do you realise he's disappeared? Somebody's stolen him."

Starkly, Seb put the facts about the Winters.

"Yes, I heard they'd been in trouble," was all Jefferson said.

"And we reckon Loner's here."

"You mean you think I employed the Winters to capture a wild dolphin?" he said scornfully.

"Something like that."

Jefferson shrugged. "You really have the wildest ideas, don't you? Particularly after you allowed this young man to break in here."

There was silence in the pool, broken only by the lazy splashing of the dolphins.

"But I've decided not to press charges," said

Jefferson suddenly. "It may not affect the police case, but —"

"Why?" asked Seb. They were all amazed at this latest unpredictable move.

"Because I believe he set out not to steal anything, but to see what I was up to. I s'pose the rest of you couldn't get anything on me, so young Tim took the initiative. Maybe I would have done the same thing at his age. In fact I wouldn't mind coming into court and speaking up for him."

Tim stared at him. He just couldn't believe what he was hearing. It was a relief, of course. A tremendous relief. But it was also so utterly, unbelievably unlikely.

"There's something else I have to tell you, although why I should after all the accusations you've hurled at me —"

"What is it?" interrupted Anne sharply.

"I have to confess I was put in a very awkward position."

"What do you mean?"

"The Winters. They thought they'd make a quick buck and fetch me a dolphin."

Tim felt a sudden choking sensation. Was Loner here or wasn't he? What game was Jefferson playing with them?

"What the hell are you on about?" breathed Seb.

"They took your dolphin – and handed him over to me."

"Why on earth didn't you say so before? Where is he?" asked Anne feverishly.

"Back in the sea. I put him back in the harbour myself, much to their fury. They threatened to beat me up so, being a coward, I gave them a pay-off. But your Loner's OK – none the worse for his experience. Last time I saw him he was heading out to sea at quite a lick."

Seb paused, unable to make up his mind. "You took him off the trawler and put him back?"

"More or less immediately."

"Didn't anyone notice?" continued Seb.

"There was one hell of a storm on, remember? Nobody much was about. It was the *North Star* that brought him in. Apparently he was dead easy to catch – very friendly. Maybe you shouldn't have made such a fuss of him."

"He's back out there?" asked Anne slowly and unbelievingly.

"He's back out there. But whether he'll stay around I don't know. He could associate this part of the coast with danger – maybe he's heading miles away."

"What made the Winters think you wanted him?" asked Seb, sounding very unconvinced.

"Because I shot my mouth off."

"In what way?"

"Saying one night in the pub how much I'd like to train a wild dolphin."

"But your publicity says –"

"I know. I'd had a few. I told you – it was my fault."

"Sam, is all this true?" Anne's voice was hesitant

but there was a light in her eyes – a light of sudden, radiant happiness.

"It's true." He was very convincing and Tim almost believed him. But what about the dolphin he'd seen in that cage? The obvious cruelty – that disgusting pool? How did all that fit in?

"Hang about." Obviously Seb was as suspicious as he was.

"Well?"

"Like it or not, Tim saw some pretty lousy conditions here – and one very battered dolphin."

"Yes, I admit that pool had got into a state, and I'm sorry. I'm having it cleaned. But that dolphin really *was* there for its own protection."

"Will you show us the cleaned pool?" asked Seb sceptically.

"Yes, when it's done. Like tomorrow. And if you're worried about my treatment of the captive dolphins – well, you can observe me for as long as you like."

"Those wretched Winters – can't they be arrested?" asked Anne.

"Definitely," said Seb.

"Isn't it enough that they've lost their boat? It's ironic, isn't it? They're probably underinsured as well." Jefferson spoke quickly and smoothly. There was a strange glint in his eye – a kind of pleasure, or was it triumph? Tim couldn't tell.

It was beginning to rain again as the members of

Green Watch left the dolphinarium and stood on the pavement outside, feeling completely indecisive at the unexpected turn of events. Only Anne seemed to have made up her mind.

"So you all believe him, do you?" she asked angrily.

"He was very convincing," began Seb.

"I know him," she replied bitterly. "I know when he's lying. Can't you see? He's playing with us like he plays with his dolphins. He specialises in degrading them – *and* us. He's always loved playing games."

"What are you trying to say?" asked Flower.

"Loner's in there," she said grimly. "I could *feel* him there."

There was a long silence.

"You're really sure?" asked Tim.

"Yes," she said quietly. "I'm certain."

"What are we going to do then?" Flower asked urgently. "Go back in there and confront him?"

"No," said Anne. "We've got to have a better idea than that. We'd better go away and think it through."

Anne came back to the caravan and Seb cooked an enormous fry-up. No one had realised how starving they were and they all ate ravenously.

When Anne thought everyone felt better she said to Tim, "During your night-time ramblings, were there any other pools in the building, except the exhibition one and that small dirty one?"

Tim spoke hesitantly. "I don't know. I didn't get

66

much of a chance to look. Remember the Rottweiler? Just because we didn't see him today —"

"OK." Seb looked thoughtful. "If only we knew the name of the box-office lady. With a bit of pressure I think she'd talk."

"Do you think she actually *knows* anything?" asked Anne.

"I'm not sure. But I've got a hunch she does."

"Ring the pub, Seb. They'd know."

"Good for you!"

Seb hurried out to the telephone box. He was gone for what seemed a very long time. During the eternal wait Tim kept thinking about Loner, swimming round and round the horrible little pool at the back.

Eventually Seb returned in triumph. "I reached her!"

"Well?" snapped Brian, unable to bear the tension.

"She's afraid, very afraid, is Mrs Anderson. She knows something's going on and she doesn't like it. She didn't like it any more when I told her she could be liable for prosecution."

"But does she *know* anything?" snapped Anne.

"She doesn't know if Loner's there. But there *is* another pool. And she's going to open it up for us."

"When?"

"Now. I know it's late but it's the only time."

"But isn't that breaking and —" began Flower.

"She's letting us in. Mrs Anderson's an employee."

"The Rottweiler?" Tim reminded them.

"We'll have to be careful," replied Seb. "But the pool is in a separate building."

"Jefferson lives over the shop," Brian pointed out.

"As I say," Seb's voice was tight with excitement and tension, "we'll have to be careful. This is going to be one of our more unorthodox missions."

"Which isn't?" asked Brian bleakly.

Chapter Seven

She was standing in the shadows in a plastic mac,
looking as if she was about to be arrested. Tim felt
most peculiar; this was the second night he was
visiting the dolphinarium after hours, but this time
more legally, or was it? Did Mrs Anderson have any
right to let them in? And anyway, it looked as if she
was having second thoughts.

"Mrs Anderson —"

"Mr Howard. I really don't think —"

But Seb was firm. "You can't let that dolphin
suffer. It comes from the wild."

"I don't even know if it's here. But he's been so
peculiar recently. And there's been men coming and
going."

"The Winters?"

She nodded. "I'm going to give in my notice. I can't stand it any longer."

Seb looked up at the windows above. "Is he up there?"

"In the flat? I wouldn't be here if he was. When he left he said he was going to a friend's for the night."

Tim breathed a sigh of relief.

"I've got all the keys because the fire officer said two people had to carry them."

"Lucky," breathed Flower.

"OK." Seb looked round. The street was quiet. "Let's go."

"We'll unlock the back yard." Mrs Anderson seemed more confident now as they trailed behind her. She walked briskly as if she were carrying out her normal duties, but her face was set and her lips were pinched. She unlocked the gate, which made a horrible screaming sound. Once they were in, they huddled in the yard hoping that no one had heard. There was complete silence and a few minutes later all three Howards began to look more relaxed. But Tim was now very afraid. Last night, tonight – so far they had been lucky not to have run into a patrolling policeman or to have attracted attention. How long could their luck last?

"Why has he got another pool in there anyway?" Seb asked Mrs Anderson.

"It's a training pool. It's connected to the larger pool by a tunnel – that's in there." She pointed to a corrugated iron construction, rusty and looking as if it might fall apart at any moment. "It links up to

70

this." She pointed to a more modern prefabricated one-storey building.

"So what's the other pool for – the one Tim saw?"

"That's for isolating a dolphin, or for special training."

"That sounds sinister," said Anne. "And why is it in such a disgusting state?"

"*Is* he cruel to them?" put in Seb quietly.

"I just don't know." Mrs Anderson was very flustered now. "Sometimes he's in a good mood and he's wonderful with them. Then, when he's in a bad one, he curses at them. I've never actually seen him ill-treat one – really. But of course I'm in the office most of the time. Trouble is, he's been so *peculiar* recently – jumpy and edgy and flying off the handle at me all the time. I don't know *what* to think. Of course I shouldn't be doing this."

She approached the door of the prefabricated building and began to fiddle around with the keys. At last she found the right one and inserted it in the lock. The door swung open noiselessly and immediately the smell of salt and fish hit their nostrils. The interior was pitch dark.

"I can't remember where the lights are," she muttered.

There was a gentle movement in the water, a splash and the sound of ripples.

"He's here!" said Anne.

Mrs Anderson eventually discovered the lights and

they found they were peering into a large round tank. The neon light made the water look very blue. At first Tim could only see a dark shape at one end, then, with a soaring dash, the dolphin leapt from the water. It seemed as if its eye was steadfastly looking at them. Then, with a neat dive, the dolphin entered the water again. Without doubt it was Loner. There was none of the docility of the captive dolphins in this one. His whole body exuded resentment at being imprisoned.

Loner swam to the side and Anne put her hand on his sleek head. He nuzzled up against her, his eye fixed yearningly, inquiringly, on hers. Tim felt his own fill with hot tears. It was the most moving sight he had ever seen.

"So it's true," said Mrs Anderson sadly.

"This is Loner." Anne continued to fondle his head. "He's in captivity – can't you see?"

"Yes," said Mrs Anderson quietly. "I can see."

"The question is," said Brian, "what are we going to do about him? How can we get him back to the sea?"

"I can arrange that." Seb was confident. "The pressure will be so great on Jefferson to return him —"

"Can he claim him?" asked Anne, her voice trembling.

"No, there are conservation laws against him doing that. Under the Wildlife and Countryside Act dolphins are protected in our waters and the Department of the Environment would come down on him very heavily indeed."

"So he'll be forced to put him back."

"He may try to claim Loner's an imported dolphin. Unless there's some way of —"

"But Loner wouldn't last that long." Anne's voice was despairing. "He'll die."

"How do you know?" asked Mrs Anderson anxiously.

"Look at him," whispered Anne.

And when they looked at him more closely they could easily see why. There were marks on his body already.

"He's been hurling himself against the sides." Anne turned to Seb. "We've got to get him out *now*."

"How was he brought here?" asked Tim.

"He was transferred from the inflatable pool to that," said Seb grimly.

Their eyes swivelled to the corner of the building. There was a large plastic container, just big enough to take Loner plus sufficient water to keep him immersed.

"He would have been terrified," rasped Flower. "Taken out of that watery wilderness and dumped in that."

Loner suddenly backed away from Anne, flipped round and took off at speed across the pool. To their horror, he swam full-tilt at the side and drove his head at the iron surround. There was a dull thump. He was thrown back slightly and paused – and then swam full-tilt at it again. The same dull thump echoed round the pool.

"Loner!"

He turned again, as if to make another suicidal run.

"Loner!" Anne's voice was firm and decisive.

There was a fractional pause. Then he came slowly towards her.

"We'll get you out." She began to stroke his forehead again. "We'll get you out."

"Does he understand?" whispered Flower.

"They're highly intelligent," replied Seb. "They've a brain bigger than ours – much bigger."

Then Loner began to make a sound – a series of sounds – that riveted them all, for it was so near a human voice as to make little difference. It was a kind of moaning and wailing that was really dreadful to hear.

"He's crying!" said Brian.

Tim felt almost as if he was under a spell. The wailing certainly sounded human, but it also sounded like the sea pounding on rocks, the surf running free, the waves rolling relentlessly on. It was human yet unearthly.

"Can they speak?" asked Flower suddenly.

Seb nodded. "Vowels only – they have trouble with consonants."

"Does Jefferson make them speak?"

"I expect he tries. It would make a great attraction for the public. And their hearing is so acute that if I poured a teaspoonful of water into this pool Loner could hear it, and pin-point its direction. And when a dolphin dies I've actually seen other dolphins nudge it into shore. They're amazingly intelligent."

"Can't we somehow get hold of a truck, and have

him away from here now?"

"Yes." Seb was very positive. "Whether we get done for breaking and entering or not." He gave a sideways, almost apologetic, look at Tim. "I'll organise something, but it means Anne staying with Loner. I'm afraid of what Jefferson might do if he comes back. He seems to be going off his head."

"My husband's got a removal van," said Mrs Anderson suddenly. "And I can drive it. Shall I fetch it?"

Her surprising offer startled them all and she went up considerably in everybody's estimation.

"Thanks!" Seb took her hand and squeezed it. "We really appreciate what you're doing."

"I'd better go and get on with it."

"Will you be OK alone?" demanded Flower.

"Yes – I'll see you later." She hurried out.

Anne kept stroking Loner's head and he stayed contentedly beside her.

"Mrs Anderson's gone to get a furniture van," Seb told her. "We can take him away in that."

She nodded, but Tim knew that although she had heard what Seb had said, she had not allowed it to distract her. It was as if the whole of her mind was focused into reassuring Loner.

"The sea," she said. "We'll be back in the sea. Soon. Very soon."

She took something out of her pocket and Tim saw that it was a small cassette player. She switched it on and held it down towards Loner. The music was about the sea, rhythmic, swelling, tumultuous. Loner looked up at her, his eyes trusting. Then a tear rolled down his beak.

"It's amazing!" whispered Brian. "He thinks like – like a human."

"It's the music." Seb stared at Loner. "Dolphins love music – look at him!"

Another tear rolled down as Anne went on stroking his wet forehead.

"Dear Loner," she murmured affectionately.

The music continued and Tim could hear the spray lashing in its soaring melody. He was so entranced that, like the others, he never heard the door opening.

"Don't move! Any of you," said Sam Jefferson softly.

"Hell!" said Brian succinctly as they all turned towards Jefferson – all except Anne, who went on stroking Loner.

"Put it down." Seb was calm.

Tim looked at Jefferson in horror. There was something in his hand and he suddenly realised with a stab of fear that it was a gun.

"What are you doing?" Jefferson's voice was thick and it was all too clear he had been drinking heavily.

Seb began to walk towards him.

"Keep back!"

"Put it down."

"I said – keep back!"

Seb went on walking towards him.

"I'll kill you!"

"You won't – you're too drunk."

"Stay where you are!"

"No chance."

Seb hurled himself at Jefferson and they went down on the floor. The gun went off with a terrific blast and Tim turned round immediately, half-stunned, desperate to see the effect on Loner. It was disastrous. He had moved into the middle of the pool and was rushing at the sides again.

"Stay still!" Seb was pinning Jefferson down. "If you move, I'll hit you again!" Tim glanced across at them. Jefferson's mouth was bleeding and Seb had the gun. He put the safety catch on.

"Anne, take this and put it in that far corner. Now."

"Right."

There was thud after thud as Loner hurled himself against the side time and time again.

"I've got to stop him!" Anne jumped into the pool and swam over to Loner. She grabbed him but he simply went on hitting his head against the side, with her struggling on top. "Help me!" she screamed.

Brian, Flower and Tim threw themselves into the pool instinctively, without communicating or think-ing. Loner would probably kill himself unless they could restrain him. They swam fast towards him and Anne.

"Hang on to him. Try and stroke him as well."

The cassette player had fallen on to the ground, but

it was still playing the magnificent oceanic theme. But Loner wasn't listening any more, and as they wrestled with his slippery body in the water Tim wondered how long they could prevent him from destroying himself.

Finally, after he had hit himself against the side a few more times, even with them all clinging to him, Loner suddenly stilled.

"Stroke him!" gasped Anne. "For God's sake, stroke him."

They all tried to as best as they could, although the pool was deep and they were out of their depth. Gradually they could feel Loner relaxing. Then he rolled over on his back, tipping them all off, seemingly exhausted.

"He'll be OK for a bit," said Anne. "Quick! We must help Seb."

They swam to the side. Seb was still sitting on Jefferson, pinning him down. To his amazement Tim saw that Jefferson was smiling. Why? wondered Tim. Why?

He soon found out. Jefferson gave a piercing whistle and the Rottweiler bounded through the door.

"The pool – get back in it!" yelled Seb.

They froze, the Rottweiler sprang – and pounced on Seb. The noise of growls and barking echoed and re-echoed round the pool as they rolled over, and to Tim's horror he saw blood pouring from Seb's hand. But Anne had already reacted. She dashed for the gun, grabbed it and ran back to Jefferson, who was sitting up nursing his injured mouth.

"Order it off – or I'll shoot you through the foot!"

He laughed. "You'd never do that, love."

She pulled off the safety catch. "Now!"

"No way."

The sound of the shot was deafening, and the Rottweiler sprang away from Seb to lie quivering and snarling softly on the floor.

"You've shot me!" Jefferson said melodramatically.

"I've nicked your toe." Anne grinned. "Take a look if you don't believe me."

He stood up, trying his foot, while she covered him. Then he sat down again. Suddenly he had sobered up considerably.

"Call the dog to you."

"Rocky! Here, boy!"

"Make him sit down."

"Sit!"

The Rottweiler sat, panting and whimpering.

"You OK, Seb?"

"Just my hand." Seb was binding it with a handkerchief. "I'll be fine. How's Loner?"

"He's OK," said Anne. "He didn't react so badly that time."

"I'll get you, Howard, if it's the last thing I do!"

"You got a licence for that gun?"

"Yes, and if I surprised intruders —"

"You wouldn't be in the clear." Seb was firm.

"So there's no point in either of us calling the police."

"Probably not. But you drew a gun on us —"

Jefferson looked at Tim. "All right, sonny. I'm still not pressing charges."

"Thanks," muttered Tim, ashamed at the relief he felt.

"That's big of me, isn't it, Anne?" Jefferson sounded very bitter.

"It's big of you, Sam." Her voice was contemptuous.

"So you're going to steal the dolphin?"

"After you denied you had it?" she said. "We're not *stealing* anything."

"No?"

"*You* stole him. From the sea. But you'd never have tamed him."

"He'd have been happier with me," replied Jefferson. "The sea's a miserable place for a lone dolphin."

Tim wondered for a moment if he was lying. But then he realised instinctively that Jefferson was telling the truth – that he really wanted power over the dolphins. He must be an incredibly lonely man, Tim thought with a sudden burst of perception.

"You must have the most incredible ego," began Seb.

"No," said Anne. "He really believes he can make them happy, don't you, Sam?"

But Jefferson wasn't listening. "I suppose Mrs Anderson turned traitor," he said angrily, rubbing at his toe pathetically. "It must be her. She's got the only other set of keys. She must have let you in."

"No comment," replied Anne.

"If it hadn't worked out," said Jefferson, "I'd have put him back."

"He'd have been dead by then!" Anne shouted.

"Nonsense – he'd have been happier with me than —"

"Didn't you see him flinging himself at the sides all the time? I never want to see you again," she said grimly. "Do you understand?"

"You won't get rid of me as easily as that," he said quietly.

Jefferson watched Anne steer Loner into the container. She continued stroking him as Seb, Tim, Brian and Flower slowly manoeuvred the container into the back of the furniture van which was parked in the yard. When they were ready to go, he strolled out with one hand on Rocky's collar, continuing to watch closely, his eyes fastened on the container.

"Stay clear." Seb turned to face him. He knew his hand had been badly scratched but at least it had stopped bleeding. Fortunately that was all he had to show from his tussle with Rocky.

Jefferson gave him a slow smile. "I'm not interfering."

"I don't ever want to see you again, Sam," Anne repeated.

He shrugged. "You don't have an exclusive claim on dolphins. I love them as much as you do, Anne."

"Don't try taking a wild dolphin again, Jefferson."

Seb's voice was bitter. "Or pulling a gun on us – I could have you arrested right now."

"And are you going to?" he asked.

"Not if you stop harassing us and Loner. If you think it's some kind of challenge to try and take him, then you're sicker than I thought."

"It's to get at me, isn't it, Sam?" said Anne. "I'm beginning to think you're jealous of Loner."

But Jefferson ignored her. "It's all very gracious of you, Mr Howard, but maybe you won't go to the police because they don't take your cranky little outfit very seriously. Isn't that more like it?"

"Don't push your luck, Jefferson," said Seb furiously.

"I haven't finished with you yet – any of you." Jefferson spoke slowly and quickly. "I'll destroy Green Watch and all you stand for."

"Mr Jefferson," Mrs Anderson spoke up, "you really should watch what you say."

"Should I? You've let me down, Mrs A. It was you who let them in, wasn't it?"

"I felt it was my duty," she said primly.

Jefferson laughed derisively and turned on his heel, taking Rocky with him.

"Come on," said Anne. "Let's head for the sea."

Chapter Eight

Slowly and carefully they carried the container down the beach. Loner seemed to weigh a ton. It was just after two in the morning and Tim felt that he was going to pass out at any moment from sheer exhaustion. Once in the shallows, they hauled the dolphin out and he flopped heavily on to the stones. In the moonlight the marks on his body seemed larger and they watched him anxiously as he lay there, inert.

"Put him out into deeper water," commanded Anne. She was soaked through like the younger members of Green Watch, but none of them complained as they waded out into the surf.

Still Loner didn't move. He floated, nuzzling at them for a moment, then floated again. Anne gave him a gentle push.

"He's disorientated," she said. She gave him another push and a wave rushed over him. Then a little quiver ran through him, there was a lurch – and he was streaking out to sea, a dark shape on the water, now seen and now lost.

Seb put his arm round Anne, and Flower and Brian stared at him. Something clicked in Tim's mind. He'd had no idea that Seb liked her so much. Not in that way.

"How's your hand, Dad?" asked Flower in a tight little voice.

"Not too bad." He still kept his arm round Anne's waist, but seeing Flower still staring, she gently moved away.

"Will he be OK?" Tim asked quickly.

Anne nodded. "For the moment."

"Jefferson. What could he do?"

"I don't know. But we've got to keep an eye on him." She sounded very insistent.

Seb agreed. "I don't like it. He really hates us now."

"You think he's dangerous?" asked Brian.

"He only pulled a gun on us," snapped Seb.

"Could he pay the Winters to catch Loner again?" asked Tim.

"He might even pay them to do something else." Anne's voice had a sob in it.

"What?"

"Kill him."

Flower glanced hurriedly at her father. "What do

you think, Dad?"

"I think Anne could be right. We'll get some sleep and tomorrow I'll warn the Winters off. Tell 'em they're breaking the law. But even so —"

"Even so what?" asked Flower impatiently.

"Even if I stop the Winters, I may not be able to stop him."

"I've got an idea," said Flower.

"What's that?" asked Anne.

"We should have thought of this before we put him back."

"Well?"

"Couldn't we take him further down the coast? Miles further? So he'd be out of Jefferson's way?"

"It *might* work. But I think he'll just swim back. He likes it here."

"It's you," said Tim.

"Me?"

"He's really fond of you." He frowned as the others laughed. "I mean it."

"I know you do," said Anne. "And I suppose it could be true. Don't forget how intelligent they are."

"But are they capable of *love*?" cut in Flower.

"Yes, I think they are," replied Anne. "We're still finding out about dolphins, and the more we discover, the more they surprise us."

Tim woke up suddenly. He had heard something. But what was it? Outside? Inside? The sound came again – a kind of light crunching. He knelt up on his bunk and peered outside – nothing. He looked at his watch. Half past three. The sound came again and again. It was probably a wandering cow – there was a herd grazing in the field next door. He'd slip out and see what was happening without waking the others.

As he opened the door he heard the crunching again and then a slighter sound, like a grunt or a sigh. It was strange, oddly human, and not at all like a cow. His curiosity outweighing his fear, Tim ran lightly down the steps into the field. Seb had rented it from a local farmer so there were no other caravans there. Neither was there a cow. They were all behind the wire; dark shapes, heads down, lips munching. Could this have been what he heard? Maybe it was. He looked round again. But there was nothing. Or was there? Surely – surely somebody was hiding behind the caravan? Yes, he was sure they were. Slowly, Tim began to walk towards them.

He didn't get very far. Suddenly a hand that stank of vinegar was wrapped round his mouth and a muscular arm encircled his waist. Tim kicked and struggled but it was hopeless. The grip was like iron. The voice was slurred and rasping.

"OK, sonny – stop struggling or I'll break your arm!" In a second he had shifted his grip and had Tim's arm in an agonising half-nelson.

Tim stopped struggling. As he did so, he was conscious of the other shadows emerging from behind the caravan. He was almost sick, partly through fright and partly through the vinegar.

"Watch this, sonny!" said his captor and gave a drunken giggle. They were all quite young – local

86

yobs and none of them sober. Then he saw they had spray-painted a slogan on the side of the caravan in huge letters: GREEN PRATTS GET OUT. And in smaller letters underneath DOLFINS ENJOY DANCIN FOR SAM.

He's put them up to it; Jefferson's probably paid them to do it, Tim thought. But more was to come. Four of them grabbed the underside of the caravan and began to push. The caravan listed slightly. Grunting, they pushed again and the caravan tilted a little more. Tim kicked out and caught his captor on the shin, but his arm was simply jerked up even more until tears of pain started from his eyes. Then, to Tim's horror, the entire caravan started to keel over and with a rending crash turned on its side. Other noises followed as small objects fell and smashed inside.

"Let's go," said one of them.

Tim's arm was wrenched again and then dropped. The onrush of relief was incredible as his captor turned and ran. As Tim staggered towards the upturned caravan he heard the sound of motor-bike engines roaring. They were getting away, but he was too concerned about the other members of Green Watch to bother about that.

As he raced towards the door, Seb poked his head out.

"What the hell —"

"Pack of yobs. All drunk."

"You OK?"

"Yeah, but what about the others?"

He heard Seb shouting their names and to his relief they all answered. Soon they were clambering out, indignant, shaken, bruised, but otherwise all right.

"It's action-packed, isn't it?" said Flower.

"What is?" said Tim stupidly.

"Life with Green Watch."

"Never a dull moment," replied Seb. Now let's get this wreck the right way up."

After half an hour of heaving, Green Watch had to admit defeat.

"We'll have to get a crane," said Seb. "And that'll cost a bomb." He caught sight of the graffiti. "I see. This is Sam Jefferson's work, is it?"

Tim nodded. "I'm sure it is."

"We've really hurt his pride, haven't we?" Anne's voice was so angry that Tim could almost feel the force in it.

"He's not putting the frighteners on us," said Brian stolidly.

"I've got a tent if I can find it." Seb clambered back into the caravan.

Ten minutes later it was pitched and they crawled inside. Then Tim popped his head out again. "Seb, Anne – aren't you coming in?"

"No," Seb replied. "We'll keep watch."

"But —"

"Go on, get some sleep."

"Seb?"

"Yes?"

"I'm sorry."

"What for?"

"I made a mistake. Again. I should have called you – not gone out on my own."

"You had some guts to do it."

"But if we'd *all* gone out, maybe —"

"There'd have been a fight. And we'd have got really hurt. So stop worrying and get some sleep. Now."

"OK." He crawled back inside the tent. But none of them could sleep immediately and all three lay there, still shocked by what had happened. Then, as Tim began to doze, he heard Seb and Anne talking quietly outside. There was something about the way they spoke that was very intimate – as if they were totally absorbed in each other. Awake again, Tim took a quick look round the tent. Brian was snoring but Flower was sitting bolt upright.

"What's the matter with you?" he hissed.

"Nothing," she snapped and lay down, pulling her sleeping bag over her head.

But Tim knew what the matter was.

"Where's Seb?" asked Tim sleepily, as he fumbled his way out of the tent to find Brian and Flower trying to make breakfast over a one-ring stove, salvaged from the caravan.

"Gone to the Winters," said Flower sharply. "With *her*."

"Her?"

"That Anne."

"Why *that* Anne? Don't you like her?"

"She was all right before Dad started fancying her."

"He doesn't —" Tim began feebly, but Flower took no notice.

"He *does*. Didn't you hear them last night?"

"This morning!"

"Don't be picky."

"It doesn't *mean* anything, Flower. They're just friends."

"Just good friends?" she suggested sarcastically. "She'll end up marrying him."

Tim put his mug down and looked up at her hot, anxious face.

"Flower?"

"What?"

"S'pose she did, would it be so bad?"

"It would be terrible."

"Why?"

"What about Mum? I still see her when I'm not on Green Watch missions."

"Aren't they divorced?"

"Yes."

"But then —"

"Oh, he's *free* to marry. Free enough."

"Then —"

"But what about Mum?"

"Well, she left him, didn't she?"

"It's not fair though, is it?"

"Why?"

"Mum was – is a gentle person. She couldn't cope with Dad's ego. They clashed all the time. We were little then. It's different now. Now Anne turns up – it's not fair on Mum."

"Flower —" Tim broke off. He couldn't face telling Flower what he really thought – that Anne was threatening Flower's own position, not her mother's. She had been the only woman in Green Watch for so long.

"I don't want to talk about it any more," snapped Flower.

"You should." He wondered what Brian felt – just how well he really understood his sister. He had said nothing, just continued to concentrate on frying bread.

"Well, I can't. Come on. Let's try and clear out the caravan. They'll be back soon."

"We can't get all the stuff out," said Brian mildly.

"We can try," she replied fiercely.

"Why?"

"I'm not having *her* coming back here and finding we've done nothing. We've got on pretty well without her, and we can go on doing so. I s'pose she reckons she can take over everything we do as well as dive and frolic about with dolphins. OK, so she thinks she's special. But she's not."

Flower ended her tirade by walking over to the caravan and, with an old rag, trying to rub out the graffiti which, of course, she soon found impossible. Suddenly Tim felt desperately sorry for her.

Forty minutes later, Seb arrived with a mobile crane and its gloomy-looking driver. An hour later, the caravan was standing again, dented and still covered with its glaring graffiti. The driver made no comment. Seb paid him and he drove his crane away as if righting vandalised caravans was something he did every day.

"Where – where's Anne?" asked Flower over-casually.

"Gone back to her boat."

"I thought she was going to spend most of her time with us now."

"Why?"

"Never mind."

Seb sighed. "We were talking to the Winters."

"How did they take it?" asked Tim.

"Oh, they were sullen. But they took it." He paused. "I overheard something rather odd, though."

"What?" asked Flower sharply.

"It was before we went in. Their cottage has got a narrow alleyway running beside it. They were talking – about doing the dolphinarium."

"*What*?" they all yelled at once.

"Yes – tomorrow as far as I could make out. It's Friday tomorrow. Perhaps they bank the takings on a Friday."

"Isn't it a bit odd though?" said Brian. "I mean – one hell of a big coincidence that you came along so neatly when they were in the middle of planning a robbery?"

"I thought about that. But I reckon they were

having a very long circular conversation. When they opened the door to us they both looked exhausted. Maybe they set up the yobs – not Jefferson."

"Either way," said Flower, "what ought we to do?"

"Keep an eye on the place tomorrow."

"All day?"

"If need be."

"Will Anne help?" she asked.

"Probably. By the way, I've got news for you, Tim. We also dropped in at the police station. You know the hearing was scheduled for tomorrow?"

"Yes," said Tim miserably.

"Well, it's off."

"Off?"

"The police have dropped charges because Jefferson isn't pressing any."

"Blimey!"

"They're letting you off with a warning."

"That's terrific!" A great load slid away from Tim. Despite the fact that he knew Seb would support him, he had still been very worried. "But why?" he added. "Why did Jefferson drop the charges? He could have made things very difficult for us all."

"Maybe he likes you, Tim," Seb grinned.

"He doesn't know me – and he could have killed us with that gun. And then there's the caravan. I'm sure he did bribe those yobs."

"It takes two," said Flower unexpectedly.

"Two to what? Tango?" Seb unsuccessfully tried to lighten the atmosphere.

"To quarrel."

"You mean Jefferson – and Anne?"

"Yes. What did she do to him to make him so upset?"

"She left him."

"But why?"

"She couldn't cope with being taken over – like he takes over everything. Including dolphins."

"She can't cope with anything, can she?"

"Flower, what are you on about?" asked Seb, surprised.

"I'm just saying she's not as great as she's made out to be."

"Who makes her out to be?"

"Let's forget it, Dad. Shouldn't we call the police – tell them what happened to the caravan? Tell them what you overheard about the robbery?"

"I've already alerted them," Seb grinned. "Not that it was very easy to convince them."

"Then why should we hang about outside the dolphinarium all day?"

"I don't think they took me that seriously," replied Seb. "Jefferson was right – once you get labelled as a conservation crank, you lose credibility. So it's up to us," he said firmly.

Chapter Nine

"Do you want to come out and see Loner?" asked Anne, arriving for a late lunch.

"Great idea," said Seb. "It's a wonderful afternoon." It was; hot with a light breeze that rustled the high grasses in the field so that they were like the sea themselves.

Brian and Tim readily agreed as well but Flower said nothing. Seb turned to her. "You coming, Flower?"

"I'm tired, Dad. I think I'll stay here and read."

For Flower not to come with them was so unlikely that they all stared at her, astonished.

"Come on," said Brian. "You'll be OK once you're in the water. Besides, you shouldn't be on your own up here."

But she shook her head. "No thanks. I'll be OK tomorrow – and those yobs won't come back again."

I know why she wants to stay, thought Tim. It's Anne. She doesn't want to come because of Anne. I must talk to her again, he thought. Anne was looking at her strangely too and Tim wondered how much she had guessed.

"OK," said Seb. "We'd better go." He glanced pleadingly at Flower for the last time but she turned her head away.

"Flower's missing something," gasped Brian as they trod water, watching Loner flashing along the surface, leaping and diving, a black streak in the blue-green ocean.

"He seems friskier than ever," said Tim. It was glorious out here with the jade waves dancing towards the granite cliffs. They were about a hundred metres off shore and there was an exultancy in the air that was crisp and brave and exhilarating.

"Look." Anne pointed behind them. "Isn't that the *North Star*?" It was, chugging over the slapping wavelets in the direction of Dragon's Teeth.

"They've got diving equipment on board," Seb pointed out. "Surely they can't be bothering to get down to the *Pole Star*? There won't be much left of her."

"Maybe there's tackle on board," said Anne. "It's not that deep out there. They could easily get some of it up."

After a while they forgot the Winters and continued to play with Loner. For a while Brian and Tim took turns at riding on his back. They had never done this before but he didn't seem to mind, particularly after Anne had stroked and encouraged him. For Tim the experience was amazing, as Loner tore through the water, strong and streamlined. All he could see as he rode was soaring spray, translucent in the cobalt blue of the sky.

At last they quietened down and drifted on the surface, utterly relaxed, while Anne took a waterproof cassette out of her wet suit. This time she played quieter music.

"What is it?" Seb asked.

"Brahms," Anne replied. "He always likes Brahms when he's a bit tired."

And it was true, for Loner had turned stomach up and was floating dreamily, as relaxed as anyone else.

On the way back in *Lady Lucy*, Tim noticed Seb and Anne talking together in the wheelhouse and he wondered if they were discussing Flower. Both seemed worried. He looked at Brian, who winked. As they were both in the stern Tim thought it safe to ask:

"Why didn't Flower come?"

"Don't fish," said Brian. "You know why."

"Are they going to get married then?"

"Don't know."

"What would you think if they did?"

"I wouldn't mind. Dad needs someone. He's

lonely. And I like Anne. She listens to you," he said simply.

"So why does Flower mind?"

"She's very close to Mum. I mean – so am I, but Flower and Mum – they've got a really special friendship."

"She wouldn't lose that."

"No."

"So why does she —"

"It's Mum and her personality. Flower never thought they should have split up. But I think it's confused in her mind. It's something to do with her as well, with Flower herself, about her being the only woman in Green Watch. She needs time to sort herself out. That's all."

"Brian —" said Tim hesitantly.

"Yeah?"

"Thanks for talking to an outsider about it." So he did understand after all, thought Tim. Bookish, unpredictable, perfectionist that he was – he really did understand her.

Brian threw him a friendly punch. "You're not an outsider, Tim. You're part of the family."

Tim felt a surge of confidence. What on earth would he do without the Howards? "There's something else I wanted to talk about," he said.

"What?"

"Sam Jefferson. He's so weird. If he's such a nasty bit of work, why did he let me off?"

"I don't know. He *is* a nasty bit of work. He likes to own people. Maybe have people grateful to him."

Tim thought about it. "I'm not that grateful to him," he said at last.

"No, but you're a free spirit, Tim. Like us, like Anne, like the dolphins. I think free spirits make him afraid."

Flower was standing on the quayside when *Lady Lucy* came in. She helped tie her up quickly and then said urgently, "Something's happened."

Seb jumped out. "What?"

"They did it."

"Did what?"

"There was a robbery at the dolphinarium."

"But today's Thursday." Seb looked almost comically outraged.

"Maybe they guessed they could have been overheard."

Seb shrugged. "Maybe. At least it'll make for some credibility with the police." He paused. "But was anyone hurt?"

"No. Apparently Jefferson was in the office – and he handed it over."

"Were they armed?"

"He's the only witness. He says yes."

"You didn't see it?"

"I went to get some supplies in the town and there was a crowd round the place. The police were there."

"Anyone think it was the Winters?"

"Apparently they were out fishing."

"We saw them," said Tim. "In the *North Star*. But

they weren't going fishing – they were going diving."

"How do you know all this about the Winters?" asked Anne.

"Mrs Anderson. She'd picked it up from Mrs Winter. They were outraged about it – the Winters, I mean."

Seb reflected. Then he said, "Could they have robbed the dolphinarium and then made the fishing boat, saying they'd been fishing all the afternoon?"

"It's possible. But Dad – I've thought of something."

"What's that?"

"Suppose – just suppose it's all a put-up job?"

"How do you mean?"

"Mrs Anderson says one of the policemen told her they got away with an awful lot of money. I mean, is the dolphinarium *that* popular?"

"Probably," said Seb. "It's one of the town's main attractions. A week's takings wouldn't be a really enormous sum though. But maybe Jefferson's been keeping it back all summer. You could be right, Flower. If it's a put-up job – a collusion between Jefferson and the Winters – it could have been a well worked-out scheme. He must be insured, so he could claim on the insurance to pay off his overheads and stash away the loot."

Brian laughed. "What a lovely old-fashioned word."

Seb ignored him. "So, the question is – were the Winters involved or not?"

"Well, apparently Jefferson was the only one to see

the robbers, and he's hardly a reliable witness."

"I don't believe they existed," said Brian. "I reckon Jefferson faked the whole thing."

"So the Winters *weren't* involved?" asked Tim.

"Oh, yes they were. But perhaps they picked up the money some other time. Maybe last night. Or early this morning. And they put it in the *North Star*."

"Brilliant!" Seb was beside himself. "Brilliant! I bet you're right."

"But that's not all." Brian's words raced on. "While the raid was meant to be taking place, they *were* out fishing. Or at least they were out in the boat. But when they passed us, there was all that diving equipment on board."

"You mean —" began Anne slowly.

"I reckon they were going to stash all that money away in the *Pole Star* – or what's left of her."

"But the wreck might break up even more,' said Tim.

"An experienced diver would know where to put it," replied Anne. "I'm sure of that."

"So they hide it away in some watertight container, and wait till the fuss has died down. Then maybe they spend it in bits. It's like an underwater bank."

"Are the Winters divers?" asked Seb.

"Anne nodded. "They've done some. But I don't think they'll take the money in bits. There'll be a share-out later. The diving would attract too much attention. Also, I think I know why Sam's done this."

"Well?" Seb sounded impatient.

"Years ago – when we were diving together – he wanted to set up a diving school in Spain. He'd never get the money together on running the dolphinarium – not if he had to pay out the overheads. But if he could get those back from the insurance and keep a lump sum of takings, maybe this is the investment he's going to make." She paused. "What are we going to do next?" she asked. But Anne was looking at Flower in a sort of questioning way and Tim knew that this had nothing to do with what she had just asked.

Seb quickly made up his mind. "Early tomorrow morning we'll go out there and take a look. But there's something else I want to do. I'm going to the town hall later tomorrow, and I'm setting up a protection trust for Loner. I've already spoken to various bureaucrats on the phone and they're very keen, particularly when they know it's not going to cost any money. Once I know that the trust has been set up, and the locals are going to prize Loner as long as he stays here, then we'll have done our job. Now let's go back and eat."

"You lot go on," said Anne. "Flower —"

"Yes?"

"I was going to brew up a cup of tea. Will you stay and have it with me?"

"Good idea, Flower. Anne can tell you all about Loner while we three cook a really slap-up high tea."

"OK," said Flower reluctantly. "See you later then."

When Flower came back she was looking happier, and over high tea Seb made an announcement.

"I want to talk to you – and it's not about the current project, which is almost over anyway."

Tim felt a pang of loss. Soon he would have to go home, and although he wanted to see Mum – and later Dad – he knew he would miss Green Watch desperately. It had been hard enough on the other two occasions, but somehow this time it was going to be much worse.

"Anne and I – me and Anne – we're – we've been —"

Brian laughed. "Spit it out, Dad!"

"Be quiet, Brian." For one who was normally so authoritative, Seb seemed to have been reduced to stuttering inadequacy. "The point is – I – we – wanted to tell you – that – because —"

"OK," said Flower. She was frowning. "You're going to get married. Anne's already told me."

"Yes, but —"

"I still feel – unsure about it, Dad. You know how I feel – how I'll always feel about Mum. But Anne – she told me a lot about herself and how she doesn't want to be a mum. Just a friend. And maybe I'll get used to that." She paused. "There's something else as well. I'm jealous of her, I guess. Another woman coming in."

"I see. We've got to talk about it, Flower. Talk about it a lot. You musn't feel —"

"Don't go on about it now, Dad. *Please*. It'll take time, that's all."

103

He smiled uneasily and then turned to Brian. "What do you feel?"

"It's great, Dad!"

"I mean – do you like her?"

"Yes, I do."

Seb turned to Tim. "And how do you feel about a new member of Green Watch, Tim?"

"I'm not —"

"Don't start on that again," said Brian. "You're part of us, and you'll never stop being part of us. Get it?" He grinned.

"Got it," said Tim. "I think Anne's great. I hope you'll both be really happy. And she'll make a terrific new member of Green Watch."

Seb took an enormous mouthful of pork pie. He seemed to be very close to tears.

Chapter Ten

They were watching TV when Mrs Anderson started crashing on the door. It was nine and the light was fading.

"Mr Howard!" Her face was flushed and she had ridden up on an ancient bicycle, whose front wheel was still spinning as it lay on the ground.

"Yes?"

"Something awful's happened!"

"What?"

"That man Jefferson – he's taken away Miss Dudley!"

"He's —"

She gave him a screwed-up piece of paper. With grinding impatience, Seb smoothed it out while the others gathered around. Scrawled in captial letters were the words: HELP ME. HE'S TAKING ME AWAY. ANNE.

"What happened?" yelled Seb.

"I was cycling by the quayside – I like to try and keep fit – and thinking of what I was going to do for a job, now I'd left the dolphinarium —"

"Get on with it!" hissed Flower.

"When I passed *Lady Lucy* I saw Mr Jefferson in the wheelhouse. Well, I was very surprised and at first I thought I was mistaken. It was getting dark, you see, and —"

"Please!" said Seb. "What happened next?"

"I saw a hand come out of the cabin below – the porthole, do they call it? And throw this screwed-up piece of paper on to the quayside. Just as I was reading it, the *Lady Lucy* started to leave. I didn't know what to do. Should I have called the police, or —" She looked up at him helplessly. "So I came here."

"We'll go after him." Seb was immediate. "But we haven't got a boat." He looked at Mrs Anderson with desperation in his eyes. "I don't suppose you know anyone who could lend me one?"

She shook her head. "The *North Star* was down at the quayside. Maybe one of the Winters might help."

Seb shrugged. "I doubt it. But we can try. Let's get down there."

"We'll I'm damned!"

The *Lady Lucy* was moored to the quay, the dark

water gently lapping about her. Seb leapt on board and Anne came out. She looked exhausted as he plunged into a stumbling explanation.

"Yes," she said dully. "He tried to take me."

"Where is he?"

"In the cabin. Lying down."

"*Lying down*? Why?"

"I hit him. Over the head with an oil lamp. Did Mrs Anderson manage to get the note?"

"Yes, she brought it to us."

"He came on board when I was having a nap. He locked me in the cabin and started the engine. But when we got out of the harbour he came down to see if I was all right, and I was ready with my oil lamp." She laughed and then winced.

"Are you OK?" said Seb in concern.

"Sure. He didn't make a very good job of it."

"But what did he want?" rasped Seb, looking murderous.

"You *know* what he wanted. To talk. To persuade. To try to get me away somewhere where he could have power over me. Kidnapping me was like kidnapping Loner. But one thing he did tell me was very significant."

"Well?"

"He said he'd sold the dolphinarium to a property developer and made a bomb. Enough to start his diving school in Spain. And he wanted me to go with him. After all we've been through! All he's done!"

"He can't have sold it." Seb was adamant. "I looked into all this when I came down here. He *rents* the place from a company in London. He's got nothing to sell."

"I guessed as much," said Anne. "I asked him about the robbery and he said they got away with a lot of money – and that it was his loss."

"Sure." Seb grinned.

"But he was different," she continued.

"In what way?"

"Well, I really thought he seemed a lot more determined."

"Where's Mrs Anderson?" asked Anne. Seb had insisted that she came back to spend the night in the caravan, but she was still wavering and worrying about Jefferson.

"Over there. In the mac, on that bike."

Anne hurried over and kissed her. Mrs Anderson went a kind of lobster pink. "He should be arrested! He kidnapped you," she said angrily.

"He should come round soon, but if he doesn't —"

"Mrs Anderson's right," insisted Brian. "He could be charged with kidnapping, as well as doing the same to wild dolphins, setting dogs on us, pulling guns, vandalising caravans . . ."

"And like everything he does it's difficult to prove," said Anne. "The police might say I went with him willingly."

"He hit you." Flower was outraged.

"And I hit him. so I'm sure they'd see it as some kind of domestic dispute. Ah – here he comes."

Sam Jefferson stepped off the *Lady Lucy* slowly and painfully.

"It's a disgrace!" shouted Mrs Anderson, but Anne put a finger to her lips.

"I think he's got a bit of a headache," she said.

Jefferson walked up to them slowly. His eyes were dull and there was a hopeless heaviness to him. Defeat hung on him like a pall.

"You've already had what you deserve." Seb's voice was quiet. "But if you come near her again, you'll get some more."

Jefferson, however, was only looking at Anne. "You and I could have a big future," he insisted, but his voice was flat.

"I don't want it, Sam."

"You'll regret it."

"I don't think so."

"Anne —" His voice broke.

But Seb had had enough. "Come on, folks, we're off."

Mrs Anderson, however, was staring at Jefferson, who swayed slightly. "You'll be going home to an empty flat, won't you?" she said suddenly, and Tim stared at her in amazement.

Jefferson shrugged. "I've got Rocky - and the dolphins."

"I'll walk home with you and make you a cup of tea. You've behaved disgracefully, but you look terrible. You can't go on like this."

"Like what?" he asked.

"Like *this*. Trying to hang on to someone who doesn't want you."

"Mrs Anderson —"

"Well?"

"Nothing." He looked away.

"Now, do you want that cup of tea? And maybe a poached egg?"

"I —"

"Yes or no?" she snapped.

"Yes." He sighed. "You're very kind."

Anne looked at Seb urgently. But he only smiled. "Mrs Anderson, you're a wonder," he said. "A real wonder."

"He won't hurt her?" asked Tim as they walked back to the caravan.

"No," said Anne. "She's a good woman, and he needs help. She'll lecture him, of course."

But she's going to his flat – with that Rottweiler," said Flower.

"Nothing will happen to her," Seb replied. "Jefferson needs comforting. She'll do what she can and go. But Anne, until this is over, you're not leaving Green Watch's sight."

"I don't really want to." She grinned.

"And is the plan the same?" asked Brian.

"Yes. Crack of dawn." Seb stared round at them. "Maybe I'm like Mrs Anderson. Anne knows what I mean. The man's dangerous, but I don't particularly want him behind bars. In a way I'd rather he went to Spain and started his diving school. But instead we're going to shop him, and if the stuff is there he could go away for a long time."

"Isn't that for the best?" asked Flower.

"He won't benefit from prison," said Anne. "And if he could only forget me he could benefit from Spain."

"So why are we diving?" asked Tim.

"Because I'm not going to stand by and condone what happened," returned Seb. "Besides, there's another factor – the Winters. They'd do anything for money and they could be a threat to Loner. And I'd definitely like to see *them* inside."

"So would we," chorused Brian and Tim.

"What do you think, Flower?" asked Anne.

"Yes, I think they should go. It's just that it must be so awful in prison."

Suddenly Tim realised that everyone was staring at him. Yes, it must be awful inside, he thought. Yet, quite soon Dad would be out again, and he wondered it after all this time he could find that difficult too.

Chapter Eleven

The next morning the weather had changed and it was raining. At 5am the first streaks of a sodden dawn were in the bulging night sky. Tim felt exhausted as they all dragged themselves out of bed, swallowed some toast and coffee and set out in the Landrover for the harbour.

"What happens if the Winters are up early?" asked Flower.

"They won't be." Anne sounded very certain. "They never start operations until about eight. There may be a few fishermen around, but they won't be interested in us. Plenty of divers go out at the most extraordinary times."

She sounded reassuring but Tim was not so sure. He felt very exposed in the Landrover, which was crammed with purposeful diving gear.

They reached the quayside and, sure enough, there was no one around at all. It was much lighter now and the rain was spitting on the tiny wave-crests. There was only a little wind, and once they had loaded *Lady Lucy* Seb took the Landrover and put it in the town car park so that the Winters wouldn't see it when they eventually emerged.

They set off about five minutes later, nudging out of the harbour. A rain mist was building up and visibility gradually worsened.

"Just what we want," muttered Seb.

As the rain pattered down, lessening slightly, the mist increased until it was like being surrounded by shifting layers of cotton wool. All sound seemed blurred and the dark cliffs behind them had long since been blotted out.

"Are we all diving?" asked Brian with sudden suspicion.

"We'll have to keep someone on deck." Seb spoke hesitantly, knowing how unpopular his decision would be.

"I'll stay then." Flower was very positive. Brian and Tim also volunteered, but in the end it was decided they would dive in relays; first of all Seb, Flower and Tim and then Brian and Anne. This seemed to satisfy everyone.

Eventually they reached the Dragon's Teeth rocks. The mist was no longer closing in, leaving them about twenty-five metres' visibility. They anchored well off the rocks, which looked small and far from menacing

113

in the dull light. The wind had dropped and the stillness was eerie.

"We'll search her systematically – it shouldn't take long. And if anything needs bringing up, we'll leave it to Brian and Anne."

A few minutes later, having put on their wet suits and tubes of air, Seb, Flower and Tim dived into the motionless sea.

It was murky below, almost as dim as the mist above, but Tim soon got used to it and was able to see more clearly as they wove their way to the sea bed. Then he had his first shock. It was like a graveyard. The floor was littered with wrecks, some broken into unrecognisable pieces, others whole and still able to be identified as small fishing boats, trawlers and what looked like a tramp steamer. The bottom was sandy and the rocks loomed on either side – a great undersea canyon with fronds of seaweed clinging like shrouds.

They swam over the wrecks, trying to find the *Pole Star*. Fish coursed around them lazily, one large specimen, with an enormous fixed eye, staring balefully at them as they swam past. Tim felt an odd sensation of being warned away – of being a trespasser in a holy place, whose worshippers were not human. More fish with big accusing eyes swam up to them fearlessly. They looked disapproving, yet Tim knew that many divers must come here, swimming round the wrecks, intruding into the depths.

Suddenly Seb gave a thumbs-up sign and Flower

and Tim followed him along the sandy sea bed. There she was, badly holed but intact, with the familiar name *Pole Star* mistily on her bows. She was lying at a slight angle, settled snugly beside a barnacle-encrusted motor yacht. Tim could see the name *Sea Breeze* very faintly under a mound of weed. She must have been very stylish in her time, and he wondered how long it had been since she foundered. Seb beckoned them on, swimming along the *Pole Star*'s deck towards the wheelhouse.

The mist hung around them, clammy but protective, making their words flat in the dull atmosphere.

"Sam was a very intelligent person," Anne was saying. "But he always did things to extremes. Even as a child, his mother told me, he was a perfectionist. He spent hours over his homework, trying to get every last detail right."

"More than I do," said Brian.

"And me. And when we were diving he double-checked everything. He must have been the safest diver ever, and I was glad of that. But when he fell in love with me —"

"Hang on!" Brian's voice was urgent.

"What?"

"I think I heard something."

"They strained to hear, but there was only woolly silence.

"What was it?"

"I thought I heard oars. Listen."

Still silence.

"Sorry," said Brian. "I must have been —" He stopped again. "It's a sort of plashing."

"What?"

"Not splashing. Plashing. As if they were muffled – the oars, I mean."

"Sounds like pirates," she said lightly. Then she heard it herself. "Yes, it *is*. It is someone rowing. But they keep stopping, don't they?"

"I think so."

They listened again, and heard the same sound, indistinct yet gaining on them.

"What shall we do?" asked Brian.

"Stay put."

"And if it's Jefferson?"

"I'm sure it won't be."

"Sure?"

"I hope it isn't." She suddenly looked very afraid.

They searched the wheelhouse but there was nothing. Then Seb led them back outside, pointing down to the holds. The rocks had holed the *Pole Star* on her prow and her stern was relatively undamaged. One of her hatches had been ripped off and inside was a deep, dark space. As Tim swam down, he saw that he was looking into a cabin. It was very weird. There were a couple of bunks and a plastic teapot floating between them. He could see a calor gas stove and a cupboard behind it.

Seb gestured at him, indicating that he wanted him

to have a look. Tim wound his way into the tiny space, and saw that the cupboard door was open. Bracing himself against the bunks, Tim felt around the dark recesses of the cupboard. He brought out a saturated tin of sugar, dissolving tea bags, swollen, disgusting bread. But nothing else. Then he turned his attention to the stove, to the bunks and their sodden bedding – and then to the space under the bunks. There was something there – something waterproof – some kind of container. He yanked and pulled and gradually, unwillingly, it came out. The container was very heavy.

"Hi!"

It was a boy a little older than Brian who came rowing into view. He wore a thick jersey and was bronzed, even handsome, in a solid, dogged sort of way.

"Doing a bit of diving?" he asked cheerfully.

Anne nodded.

"That's the graveyard down there, isn't it? Great diving spot."

She nodded again.

"Where have you come from?" asked Brian.

"My parents have got a cruiser moored offshore. Thought I'd like a row."

"You should be careful in this mist," said Anne. "It's easy to get lost. And we're on the Dragon's Teeth. If a wind gets up you could be swept on to them."

"Not much chance now."

"Things change quickly here," she said abruptly.

Brian looked at his watch. It was almost seven. The boy was fiddling with something at the bottom of the boat. What could it be? Suddenly a chill crept over him as he remembered Jefferson's gun in the dolphinarium. Could he be in league with him somehow? The boy's accent was rough and there was a Cornish burr to it. Nothing seemed to fit in with the image of parents with a cruiser.

"I haven't seen you around in the town," said Anne, and Brian guessed that she was suspicious of him too.

"No?" He was still scrabbling around in the bottom of the boat and then he obviously found what he was looking for with a grunt of delight. Brian felt a horrible freezing sensation.

Somehow Tim dragged the container out and suddenly found Seb hovering above him, tapping him on the shoulder and gesturing to him not to open it. Then he was beside him and they were both struggling with it. Slowly they moved it from the floor, up through the shattered hatch and on to the deck. Flower signalled at them. Were they going up? Seb hesitated and then indicated that they should stay where they were while he went and checked out the surface. Slowly he began to weave his way up.

"You see – I've got a compass." He grinned at them, holding it up. "Can't get lost that easily."

Brian expelled a great sigh of relief and, looking across at Anne, saw that she was grinning at him and obviously feeling as relieved as he was.

"Wait a minute," she said, and the grin disappeared. "I can hear something else."

"What?" asked Brian, his nerves jumping again.

They both listened and the boy was quiet too.

"Oars," she said. "I can hear the sound of oars. Again."

Just as she spoke the words, Seb broke surface.

They waited for over five minutes, then seven, then almost ten before making a move. Flower signalled that she should go up and Tim stay there. But Tim shook his head. This was the last place on earth that he wanted to be on his own.

"I'll come with you," he mimed, knowing he was being feeble. She paused and then nodded. Then she pointed down at the container and signalled that they should put it back.

Without Seb it was incredibly heavy, but somehow they managed to slide it back down the broken hatch and into the cabin-cum-galley. Straining every last inch of strength they shoved it back under the bunk and swam up on to the tilting deck. Then, with a quick thumbs-up, Flower headed for the surface and Tim followed.

Lady Lucy rocked quietly at anchor. The mist was

as thick as before and the silence was only broken occasionally by the slap of a tiny wave or the creaking of the anchor chain. As they both surfaced, they saw there was no one on deck.

"Greedy pigs!" she snapped. "They're having breakfast."

"Seb wouldn't have left us down there – don't be daft," said Tim, his teeth chattering despite his wet suit.

"Perhaps we misunderstood him," she replied. "Let's go and see."

They clambered up the ladder and on to the deck.

"Dad!" she yelled. "What are you up to?"

But there was no reply, and when they hurried into the wheelhouse, and later the cabin, there was no sign of anyone at all.

"I don't get it," said Tim.

"Jefferson?" Her voice was almost a choke.

"I just don't believe it. They *must* be somewhere."

"Where?"

They went out on deck to look around again, but the silence was like a wall.

"They came for them," she said.

"What about us?"

"Maybe they'll be back."

Then they heard the sound dimly in the mist. The muffled sound of oars.

"Quick!" she said.

"Where?"

"Back in the sea. Lower yourself gently down the ladder. We'll hide on the sea bed."

"What about the air?"

"We've got twenty minutes' worth – or there-abouts. Now get going before they see us."

They swam down as fast as they could, weaving their way through the water pressure. Once on the sea bed they looked up, but could see no sign of movement above. They wouldn't see a rowing boat anyway, thought Tim – or anything else, come to that. But suppose they also took away *Lady Lucy*? How far was it to swim to shore? They would have to jettison all their heavy diving gear if they did. It was also very cold down here; as a hiding place, thought Tim, it was lousy.

They must have stayed down there for about ten minutes when Flower touched him on the shoulder, pointing upwards. Once again they both wove their way to the surface and emerged spluttering, expecting to find *Lady Lucy* gone, or heavily occupied by Jefferson and the Winters. But there was no sign of anyone and, for the second time, they clambered back on board. Flower and Tim wondered what on earth was happening. They had definitely heard the muffled sound of oars.

"Look!" hissed Flower. She had crossed to the other side of the boat and when Tim joined her he could see the rowing boat, gently bobbing up and down, her painter tied to a small stanchion on the deck of *Lady Lucy*.

"Who?" whispered Tim.

121

She raised a finger to her lips and tiptoed towards the wheelhouse. When Tim drew level with the window, he felt a sudden stab of shock. The boy was sitting there asleep, his chin buried deep on his chest.

"Who's he?" Tim asked stupidly.

"Never seen him before."

"But what's he doing?"

"Sleeping, by the look of it."

"Here?" Tim was outraged and Flower gave a nervous giggle. The boy woke with a start and turned to stare at them with equal amazement. Quickly Flower shed her breathing tube and Tim did the same. It was an instinct. A preparation.

"What are you doing here?" asked Tim abruptly. The boy just stared at him.

"You're on our friend's boat. And where is she?"

"Where's who?"

"Anne. Anne Dudley."

"Don't know her."

"But what are *you* doing here?" Tim stepped forward aggressively. The boy was bigger than him, but if it came to a fight . . .

"Yes," said Flower. "Explain yourself. Now." Despite himself, Tim smiled. She sounded frightfully headmistressy.

"I saw the boat was deserted so I came on board."

"And went to sleep?"

"I was knackered. I rowed from my parents' boat – it's about a mile away."

"In this mist?" asked Tim sceptically.

"I've got a compass."

"And you calmly came on board and went to sleep?"

"I told you – I was knackered."

"I don't believe you," said Flower.

"Please yourself," said the boy rudely.

"Where are they?"

"I told you —"

"Who took them?" Flower was within centimetres of him now. "Where's my father? Where's Anne? And my brother? What's happened to them all?"

"It's nothing to do —"

"It's everything to do with me!" She suddenly slapped him hard round the face and he staggered back.

"Don't you touch me!"

"Where are they?"

"I told you. I'm not going to —"

She hit him again and he fell back against the wheel. Thoroughly infuriated, the boy launched himself at Flower, swinging punches. With great agility she dodged them, and Tim waded in. Before either of them could make contact, the boat lurched and they fell in a heap on the floor with Flower on top. As they did so, the boy gave a sudden howl of excruciating pain and Tim and Flower rolled off him.

"My wrist!"

Tim was poised, wondering if he was faking.

"I've broken my wrist – I'm sure I've broken my wrist!"

His face was white under its tan and beads of sweat had come up on his forehead. The boy just lay there, his wrist splayed out in a horribly unnatural position.

"I'm sorry." Flower and Tim hovered over him helplessly, unsure of what to do next.

"It hurts like hell!"

"If you hadn't —" But Tim's voice died away. It wasn't the time for recriminations now.

"We'll get it fixed." Flower's voice was hesitant.

"How?"

"We'll take you back to the harbour – or your parents' boat."

The boy didn't reply, but just lay there rather pathetically.

"I can tie it up for you," she pressed. "Make it a bit more comfortable. I've done a first aid course."

"Could you?" He sat up with difficulty and looked at her hopefully, wincing as his injured wrist moved.

"There's a condition."

"What?"

"Tell us the truth. Now."

The boy stared at her without speaking.

"Now," said Flower, her voice grindingly hard.

"All right."

"Fast."

"The Winters took them. They'll be back soon."

"Are they hurt?"

"No. The bloke got a bang on the head. But I guess he'll be all right."

"Who are you?"

"Kenny Beck."

"Are you . . . in on what the Winters are doing?" Tim asked abruptly.

"I don't know what the hell they're doing, but they wanted another diver. That's me."

"What for?"

"To get something down there – in that wreck."

"We know."

"I'm their cousin – live up the coast a bit. Unemployed. The whole family's out of work. They offered me some diving – that's all. They'll pay me. I'm just to help and keep quiet."

"Where's my dad?" Flower's voice was soft and menacing.

"They took them all to the lighthouse."

"The lighthouse?"

"It's deserted now —"

"What are they going to do with them?"

"Don't know."

"Didn't you realise they were up to no good?" demanded Tim.

He looked away. "They gave me money. A lot of money."

"To shut you up," said Flower bitterly.

He nodded.

"Come on, Flower," said Tim sharply. "Don't string it out. Let's decide what to do."

"I *know* what we're going to do," she replied crisply.

"What?"

"We're going back in the water – and we're going to bring that money up before anyone else gets it."

"Blimey! You sure this is the —"

"Then we're going to the lighthouse."

"What about —" Tim was astounded. Was she really prepared to take such a risk?

"This boy? What's your name again?"

"Kenny," he said meekly.

"You'll have to stay here."

"How long you going to be?"

"As long as it takes."

"Wait a minute," said Tim. "Do they know we're here?"

"The bloke – your dad – they knocked him out."

"What?" rapped out Flower.

"It's all right. He's OK. And he didn't shop you. When he came round he said you two were back home, and he was the only one diving."

"And they believed him?"

"I dunno. Maybe. But they left me here to check. I was supposed to report back if no one appeared, but I fell asleep —"

"So they might turn up at any moment," said Flower.

"S'pose so."

"Then we're going to have to put you in one of the bilges."

"That's nice."

"One of them's empty. Anne uses it as an extra larder. We're going to put you in there. Gagged."

"My wrist —"

"We'll be careful."

"You'd better be."

"Then if they come," said Flower. "They'll think you've gone away."

"What about the rowing boat?" asked Tim.

"Where's that axe? I know there's one on board."

"It's in the galley. What are you going to do?"

"Sink the boat."

"Bits will float."

"All right – better still, set it adrift."

"What happens if they find it?" asked Tim, trying to keep abreast of every eventuality.

"They'll be worried, if they care about him at all." She stared at Kenny. "You ready?"

"If you're careful."

Gingerly they began to help him down.

"Let's go."

"Hang on —"

"Why?"

"Look at that."

There was a sudden slap of water and out of the depths rose Loner.

Chapter Twelve

Loner swam around the boat and then came to rest at the bottom of the ladder. He watched Tim and Flower putting on their new air cylinders and then moved over as they clambered down the ladder. They stroked him as they entered the water and, as they dived, the dolphin dived with them.

Underneath vision was clearer now and they swam over the graveyard, Loner streaking between the wrecks, heading for the surface, breaking through and then diving down towards them again. Eventually they reached the *Pole Star*.

Flower beckoned Tim down towards the black hole of the cabin and they wrested the heavy container from under the bunk and up on to the deck again. But without Seb's help, the container was incredibly heavy, and each time they tried to lift it from the deck it felt as if their arms were dropping off. They tried again and again, but it was no good and the pain seared their arms, reminding them how hopeless it all was.

They stood on the tilting battered deck, staring at each other hoplessly while Loner swam around them, wondering if it was a game. Again they tried to lift the container, and again failed miserably. Then Loner swam down towards it and nudged at it with his beak. It lifted – and fell on its side.

Suddenly Tim knew what they had to do, and when he looked at Flower he realised she knew too. If they could get Loner to help, if they swam either side of him, maybe he could balance the container on his back. Stroking him, Flower pointed to the container and he nudged at it again. Together, with more optimism, they heaved, and suddenly Loner came under it, taking the weight on his back while Tim and Flower struck out on either side. With Loner gliding between them, they began their incredible journey up towards the surface. The graveyard lay below them, its wrecks gathered in silent gloom, and its pop-eyed fish staring upwards in apparent amazement at the extraordinary convoy above them. It was as if they were carrying some holy grail, thought Tim, and not the takings of a tatty dolphinarium.

Slowly, they wove their way up to the surface. When they broke through, the mist had receded a little and a pale sun glinted in the sky. They swam on and Tim felt as if he and Flower were part of Loner.

"Get it to the ladder and then we'll lever it up."

It took ten minutes for Tim and Flower to struggle up with it, but in the end they made it and took off their cylinders. Then they both climbed back down the ladder and, tired as they were, spent five minutes stroking Loner. He kept diving down and returning to the ladder. After a while, Flower realised what he wanted.

"He thinks it's a game," she said. "He wants to do it all over again."

"I don't," said Tim firmly.

Eventually they climbed back on the deck again and lay there exhausted.

"We should get Kenny out," said Flower.

"In a minute." Tim felt like going to sleep. "Can you handle this boat?"

"I think so. We mustn't relax, Tim. Dad and Brian and Anne could be in real trouble."

"We'll go to the lighthouse and rescue them."

"You make it sound too easy."

Tim sat up. "Let's get Kenny out."

Although his wrist was hurting a good deal, Kenny seemed to be none the worse for his temporary imprisonment. He didn't seem to bear them any ill will for shutting him up, and even told them that as far as he could tell no one had approached the *Lady Lucy*.

"What now?" he asked as they helped him down into the cabin.

130

"How's the wrist?" asked Flower.

"Lousy."

"I'm sorry – I think we have to go to the lighthouse first."

"First?"

"Before we get you medical treatment," she said hesitantly.

He nodded. "Has this boat got a radio?"

"No."

"Pity. I thought you could have got me lifted off."

"I'm sorry." Flower's concern was quite genuine.

"It's OK. I'll survive. Just keep me out of any rough stuff."

"Will there be any?" asked Tim doubtfully.

"Depends where the Winters are," replied Kenny ominously.

"And Jefferson?"

"I think you'll find he'd do anything to keep away from the Winters. They've really fallen out in a big way, you know."

Flower and Tim exchanged glances. This could be useful.

"This lighthouse. Any radio there?" asked Flower.

"No. It's derelict. There's an automatic beacon on shore now."

"So – there'll be no outside help."

"Not that I know of," replied Kenny.

"Loner's following us."

"Who?"

"A dolphin we know," explained Tim to Kenny casually.

"Blimey! Let's take a look."

Flower stayed at the wheel while the boys went to the stern and watched Loner capering along behind them in the wake of a stream of gulls.

"Do you know this lighthouse?"

"A bit." Kenny winced, his shoulders tense. Flower had put his wrist into a sling, but although it was hurting less it was still very painful.

"What's it like?"

"Nothing much to it. Bit of rock and the building." Kenny paused. "That the money you pulled out?"

"We think so. It's sealed up."

"Why not open it and check?"

Tim gazed at him suspiciously. "We thought we'd leave that to Seb."

"Where you put it?"

"In the – hang on, why do you want to know?"

"Just curious."

"Oh, yeah?" said Tim aggressively. "You're still working for *them*, aren't you? You still want your share."

"We need it. At home."

"So you'd do anything for it."

"What do you mean?" There was anger in Kenny's voice now.

"Do somebody over for it?"

"No." He laughed, and some of the anger faded. "I'm not that much of a fool."

"You sure? You really sure you would stop at that?"

"I'm sure." He gazed down at Loner, gliding and diving through the smooth sea. "He's free, isn't he?"

"He is now. The Winters kidnapped him, you know."

"I heard about that. Didn't realise it was this one, though."

"Well, it was."

They were silent, watching Loner's graceful progress.

"Mist's lifting," said Kenny softly.

"Pity."

"You can see the lighthouse. Just."

Tim craned forward. He was right; it could just be seen as a dim outline in the mist. He shouted to Flower, but she had seen it too.

"Can't see any sign of the trawler."

"Maybe they're out looking for me," said Kenny rather wistfully.

"We'll have to put you back in the bilge again," replied Tim with sudden decision.

"But I —"

"No." Tim was ruthless. "Why should we trust you?"

He shrugged. "No reason."

The lighthouse was still intact – a long tubular shape on seaweed-hung rocks. A flight of stone steps led up from a jetty and there was a large iron door that looked impenetratably fastened. There was still no sign of any life as *Lady Lucy*, accompanied by Loner, nestled up to the jetty in the windless morning.

"What shall we do?" asked Tim, suddenly feeling helpless.

"One of us will stay with the container and keep a lookout," Flower began. "We'd better toss for it." She flipped a coin. "Heads you go, tails I go," she said.

Tim looked down as it fell on to the table. It was heads. He gazed across at the iron door. "What shall I do if it's locked?" he asked. "Climb the walls?"

"You could try," was the enigmatic reply.

Chapter Thirteen

The wind came, teasing, mounting as Tim walked up the smooth, weed-hung steps. The mist began to part, its last strands slipping over the top of the lighthouse.

Tim went up to the door; it was locked, immovable. Disconsolately, he wandered round the side and found a small circular window. The glass had been broken and it was boarded up, but when he rattled at it, he felt the plywood move. He wrenched at it, discovering that it was easy to pull out. It left a space which, Tim reckoned, if he put his mind to it, he could wriggle through.

At first it was very difficult but, grimly determined, he pushed on until, with a smothered cry of anguish, he fell through on to a hard, dusty stone floor. The whole place smelt horribly shut-in and for a minute or so he lay still, not daring to move. In front of him, Tim could see a flight of steep, circular stone steps. Staggering to his feet, he began to climb them.

It sounded like the sea, then it sounded like a slumbering giant, then the wind, then the hissing of a snake. Tim stopped, trembling. The sound was magnified in the stairwell and rose and fell with a terrible regularity. What could it be? For a moment his imagination told him that something was concealed in the lighthouse, something had taken it over. An elderly sea monster? A sea serpent of some sort?

Tim shuddered as he climbed on towards the sound, which became louder and louder. The stairs seemed endless, steeper, more exhausting, until at last he came to the top. Round one more corner, and he was standing in a bare circular room with a great white space on the floor. It must have been where the light had stood. The walls were of glass and he had a panoramic view of ocean and shoreline. The sound of the monster – or whatever it was – was much louder and there was a slight wheeze to it. He looked up to see another flight of steps leading even more steeply upwards.

The Rottweiler lay stretched out in the centre of a small room that might once have been sleeping accommodation. Seb, Anne and Brian were bound and gagged in a rough semi-circle against the wall, and, to Tim's intense surprise, so was Sam Jefferson. Their eyes glowered at him in the gloom and their expressions were stabbingly intense. Were they trying to warn him against something? The Rottweiler? Suddenly the dog opened one eye. It was bloodshot. Tim froze; his heart seemed to be bigger than his body and the pulse was like a hammer. But the Rottweiler didn't move. The eye closed and the heavy breathing resumed. This was what he had heard – the Rottweiler breathing. Why was it so sluggish? Very gingerly he moved forward and then, hardly daring to look, he stepped over its out-stretched body.

In a few seconds he was at Seb's side. He removed the gag and began to fumble at his bonds.

"Good for you!" Seb's voice was hoarse and dry.

"What's up with the dog?"

"It's doped."

"Why?"

"Jefferson had it with him on the trawler – the *North Star*. They always intended to jump him, I suppose. Doped the dog first." He looked across at him, and Sam Jefferson shrugged. "They rowed across and held us up with a gun. I'd only just surfaced and got knocked out. I think the Winters were in favour of knocking us all unconscious and scuppering the *Lady Lucy* with us on board. But Jefferson was still in charge then, and persuaded them to take us to the *North Star*. I managed to convince them that we'd already got the container

137

and you and Flower were taking it back to land while we checked on the dolphin."

"So that's why they've left you here – racing after us."

"They haven't left us," said Seb drily. He rose shakily to his feet as Tim finally undid his ankles. "One of them is downstairs."

"What? I didn't see him."

"There's a cellar under the lighthouse with a kitchen. No windows – maybe he didn't see you."

"Maybe," replied Tim uneasily, moving over to release Anne.

"I expect the other one'll be back soon, empty-handed."

"We've got the container," said Tim proudly. "We brought it up with Loner's help."

"*Loner*?"

"He turned up, and helped us up with it."

"He's marvellous, isn't he?" said Anne affectionately.

"Where's Flower?" said Brian as Tim released him.

"On *Lady Lucy* with Kenny."

"*Kenny*?"

"The boy – the cousin of the Winters."

"Oh, him. I was wondering where'd he'd got to."

"They sent him back in case we reappeared. We had a bit of a fight with him. He's broken his wrist."

"I see." Seb grinned. "You two seem to have been pretty resourceful."

Tim was undoing Jefferson now while the others

138

were rubbing their wrists and ankles.

"Thanks." Sam Jefferson stood up. "I should never have trusted the Winters," he said, "They'd probably planned to do me all the time." He paused. "I've been a fool – the only thing I can do now is change sides." He laughed emptily. "Will you have me?"

Seb nodded. "I can't trust you, but I've no choice."

"I'm sorry to have put you in such danger," Sam went on, looking hard at Anne.

"You saved our lives," she said quietly.

"I bought you time, that's all. But I want you to do me a favour." He was looking at Tim now.

"What kind of favour?"

"Throw that money away – somewhere deep. I don't want it. Let it remain one of those unsolved mysteries." His gaze shifted to the Rottweiler and he went over and knelt down beside it.

"Rocky," he whispered. The dog stirred and stood up shakily. "I don't know what they gave him," he said bitterly. "But at least he's coming out of it. By the way – in case it's of any interest – I didn't pay those drunken idiots to paint all over your caravan and then overturn it. It was the Winters, but I don't expect you to believe me after all that's happened."

"I *do* believe you." Seb looked at Rocky. "He's lucky – they could have killed him."

"Wait," said Brian.

There was the sound of footsteps coming up the stairwell.

"Back on the floor – quick! Tim, get behind the door with me!"

Rocky stretched and yawned, showing long, sharp teeth.

The footsteps came on relentlessly as the others softly hurried back to their original positions. Outside the wind moaned and Tim could hear the waves lashing the lighthouse wall. He wondered where Loner was. Was he still waiting outside for them? The footsteps came nearer until Roddy Winter appeared in the doorway. He looked tired and wary – warier still when he saw Rocky's bared fangs and crouched position. He pulled out a small revolver and pointed it at the Rottweiler. But Rocky was unimpressed and crouched lower, ready to spring.

"Stay where you are, you nasty-looking brute!"

But Rocky was not in the least over-awed.

"Stay —"

Before Rocky could spring, Seb jumped from behind the door. It was all over very quickly as he karate-chopped him. Roddy Winter fell heavily, and the small revolver he had taken from Jefferson slid across the floor.

"He'll be out for an hour or so," said Seb grinning as he picked it up. But Rocky was still growling. "Call him off, Sam."

"Rocky – here, boy!"

Reluctantly the Rottweiler joined his owner.

Almost heady with relief, Tim glanced out of the window. *Lady Lucy* was bouncing up and down at the jetty. Alongside her was the *North Star*.

"She's been boarded."

"Alec's on board," said Sam Jefferson. "Where's the money?"

"In the cabin," replied Tim miserably. "And where's Flower?"

"We'll never get there in time," muttered Seb.

"You might not," said Jefferson, "but Rocky can."

"But what could he —" began Anne.

"If I say 'go search *North Star*', he'll be on it like a flash. He knows it very well, I'm afraid."

"What use would that be?"

"It'll give us time," said Jefferson. "He'll be quite safe. There was only one gun – mine," he added ruefully.

"Time's running out," replied Seb grimly. "He's got her on deck."

Tim craned his neck. Sure enough Alec Winter was holding Flower with one arm twisted behind her back. She was struggling desperately.

"What's he going to do?" whispered Brian.

"If I'm not mistaken," replied Seb, "he's going to push her in."

"Go search *North Star*!" yelled Jefferson, and Rocky bounded down the stairs in one gigantic leap.

"Come on." Seb was behind him. "We've only got seconds."

We haven't even got that, thought Tim as he watched Alec Winter throw Flower into the boiling surf. "She's in!" he bellowed.

But the others had gone.

Tim had never travelled down a flight of stairs so fast. His feet hardly seemed to touch the worn stone. It seemed only seconds before he was out on the rocks, following the others down the stone steps to the jetty. He saw Alec Winter jump from *Lady Lucy* to the *North Star*, nursing something very heavy in his arms. But there was no sign of Flower.

"There she is!"

"Blimey!"

"She's swimming, or —"

"She's not! Flower's on Loner's back!" yelled Anne in delight.

"And Winter's casting off!" shouted Brian.

"No he's not!" Seb was already leaping from one boat to the other. "He's not going anywhere!"

"Wait a minute – I'm coming!" Brian began.

"No you're not!" Seb was on the deck already. He ducked as Winter lunged at him with his powerful fists.

"Here comes Flower," said Anne, staring at the conflict on the *North Star* with horrified eyes. She was clinging to Loner's back, shivering as he piloted her into the crest-tumbling shallows. They all leaned over and pulled her in.

Then Tim saw that Sam Jefferson was also on the *North Star* and that both he and Seb were grappling with Alec Winter. A final mighty punch caught Jefferson and he fell back on the deck and lay still, but Seb hit Winter hard and he went down too.

"You OK, Jefferson?" Seb felt his pulse.

The others swarmed on to the deck of the *North*

Star as he did so, including a saturated and shivering Flower.

"Is he all right?" asked Anne, kneeling down beside him. Rocky, who had been crouching on the other side of the wheelhouse, exhausted after his long run down from the lighthouse while still partly drugged, came panting over and licked his forehead.

"He's cracked his head and cut his arm open on something." Seb ripped off part of Sam's shirt and used it to stem the flow of blood.

"Anyone left alive out there?" asked Kenny as he came out of the cabin of the *Lady Lucy*. He had a nasty bruise on his head. "Alec didn't trust me, even with a broken wrist."

Tim grinned at him. "We're OK."

"I watched through the porthole and saw that dolphin bring Flower in. It was amazing!"

"Yes, he is rather," said Flower, her teeth chattering.

Sam Jefferson groaned and tried to sit up. Seb pushed him back.

"Do me a favour," he said again.

"Well?" Seb looked dubiously at him.

"The money."

"What about it?"

"Where is it?"

"On the deck where Winter dumped it."

"Chuck it overboard."

"But —"

"Go on. Let it be like we said. Another unsolved mystery."

"It's your own money," said Seb curiously.

"Yes, I know. But it's contaminated now. I've ruined everything. Even the Winters were just ordinary fishermen before I polluted them with all this."

"What about the insurance?" said Seb quietly. "You can't claim on that now."

Sam shrugged. "I just won't fill out the forms when they come."

Seb hesitated, but Anne went over to fetch the container. "Here it is," she said. "I think Sam's right. It *is* contaminated."

"Go on – chuck it," said Sam Jefferson urgently.

Still Seb hesitated. Then he pitched it over the side.

They collected the still unconscious Roddy and put him in the cabin of the *North Star* with Alec.

"I'll take them back," said Seb. "You'll have to help me, Sam. They can't blackmail you because the situation's stalemate, and I don't think we should turn them in when it was all your fault in the first place. I think between us we can convince them to stick to fishing in future."

"I must make it right for them somehow," Sam agreed. "That's why I had to get rid of the money. To make a fresh start."

Flower had changed into an old boiler suit of Anne's

and was sipping coffee while Tim and Brian made toast. It was lunch-time and they were ravenous. Rocky lay on the floor, watching the toast, saliva running down his chin. Suddenly he didn't look so ferocious any more – just greedy.

The wind had gone down a little and the waves, although boisterous, were no longer so rough.

"We'd better get going," said Anne. "We've got casualties to get to hospital."

"Sam's coming with me." Seb finished rebandaging his arm. "It's not a deep cut. It's Kenny who's in real pain."

"Where's Loner?" asked Sam.

"Splashing about outside. Hoping we'll play with him," said Anne.

"I've got an idea," said Sam suddenly.

"What's that?"

"This Dolphin Protection Scheme. How about me helping? I could organise it. For Loner and others like him. What do you reckon?"

"You serious?" asked Seb.

"Very."

"Of course he is," said Anne. "And he's a wonderful organiser." She looked away.

"It's all right," Jefferson whispered. "I'm not making claims on you any longer. I know I've lost out."

"I'm sorry, Sam."

But this time it was his turn to look away.

"One thing," Seb asked Anne as they went up to the deck. Tim followed, hoping for a sight of Loner, and then wished he hadn't. This was their private moment, he thought, cursing his stupidity. "I've always wanted to live in a lighthouse," said Seb tentatively. "I should think I could buy it – no one seems to want it."

"That's funny," said Anne. "That's always been an ambition of mine too."

Tim leaned over the bow and watched Loner diving and gliding towards him. The dolphin looked up at him and then the gentle intelligent eye disappeared as he dived again.

MYSTERY THRILLER

Introducing, a new series of hard hitting, action packed thrillers for young adults.

THE SONG OF THE DEAD by Anthony Masters
For the first time in years 'the song of the dead' is heard around the mud flats of Whitstable. But this time is it really the ghostly cries of dead sailors? Or is it something far more sinister? Barney Hampton is sure that something strange is going on – and he's determined to get to the bottom of the mystery . . .

THE FERRYMAN'S SON by Ian Strachan
Rob is convinced that Drewe and Miles are up to no good. Why else would two sleek city whizz-kids want to spend the summer yachting around a sleepy Devonshire village? Where do they go on their frequent night cruises? And why does the lovely Kimberley go with them? Then Kimberley disappears, and Rob finds himself embroiled in a web of deadly intrigue . . .

Further titles to look out for in the Mystery Thriller series:

Treasure of Grey Manor by Terry Deary
The Foggiest by Dave Belbin
Blue Murder by Jay Kelso
Dead Man's Secret by Linda Allen
Fighting Back by Peter Beere

PRESS GANG

Why not pick up one of the PRESS GANG books, and follow the adventures of the teenagers who work on the *Junior Gazette*? Based on the original TV series produced for Central Television.

Book 1: First Edition

As editor of the brand new *Junior Gazette*, and with five days to get the first edition on the street, the last thing Lynda needs is more problems. Then an American called Spike strolls into her newsroom and announces he's been made a member of the *Gazette* team too . . .

Book 2: Public Exposure

Lynda is delighted when the *Junior Gazette* wins a computer in a writing competition. But she can't help feeling that it was all a little too easy . . . Then articles for the *Gazette* start to appear mysteriously on the computer screen. Who is the mystery writer, and why won't he reveal his identity?

Book 3: Checkmate

It's midnight, and Lynda's got to put together a whole new edition of the *Junior Gazette* by morning. The only way she can do it is to lock the office, keeping her staff in and their parents out! Spike's supposed to be taking a glamorous new date to a party – how is he going to react to being locked in the newsroom for the night?

Book 4: The Date

It's going to be a big evening for Lynda – a cocktail party where she'll be introduced to lots of big names in the newspaper business. There's only one problem: who's going to be her date? The answer's obvious to most of the *Junior Gazette* team, but Lynda is determined that the last person she'll take to the party is Spike Thomson!

THE STEPSISTERS

When Paige's Dad marries Virginia Guthrie from Atlanta, she's thrilled that he's found someone to make him happy. But how will she get on with her new stepbrother and stepsisters? Especially Katie, the beautiful blonde fifteen-year-old, who looks like a model and can charm her way out of anything!

1 The War Between the Sisters £1.75

Not only does Paige have to share her room with her stepsister, Katie, but then she finds that Jake, the boy she's fallen in love with, finds Katie totally irresistible. Paige's jealousy leads her to do some pretty stupid things to get her own back . . .

2 The Sister Trap £1.75

Paige is delighted when she gets a job working on the school magazine. Especially when she becomes friendly with the magazine editor, Ben. But her jealousies over her beautiful stepsister, Katie, flare up again when Ben starts taking a lot of interest in Katie's swimming career.

3 Bad Sisters £1.75

There's a rumour going round that Mike Lynch, the swimming champion, is cheating at school to stay on the team. And when Paige investigates the story for the school newspaper, she suspects that her stepsister, Katie, might be helping him. Should she find out the truth, even if it means getting Katie into trouble?

4 Sisters in Charge £1.75

Paige is horrified when her dad and new stepmother announce they're going away together for a week. It means that she and Katie, her glamorous, popular stepsister, will be on their own together for the first time. Taking their past difficulties into account, Paige knows it won't be easy. But things turn out even more traumatic than either stepsister had suspected!

HIPPO BESTSELLERS

Indiana Jones And The Last Crusade (story book) by Anne Digby	£2.95
Marlene Marlow Investigates: The Great Christmas Pudding Mystery (fiction) by Roy Apps	£1.75
Marlene Marlow Investigates: The Missing Tapes Affair (fiction) by Roy Apps	£1.75
Swimming Club No 1: Splashdown (fiction) by Michael Hardcastle	£1.75
Swimming Club No 2: Jump In (fiction) by Michael Hardcastle	£1.75
Beware This House is Haunted (fiction) by Lance Salway	£1.95
The Plonkers Handbook (humour) by Charles Alverson	£1.95
Knock Knock Joke Book by Scoular Anderson	£1.95
Coping With Parents (humour) by Peter Corey	£1.95
Private Lives (non-fiction) by Melvyn Bagnall	£2.50
The Spooky Activity Book by Karen King	£2.25
Christmas Fun (activity) by Karen King	£2.25